Layla's body recoiled as a bullet whizzed past her ear.

Another shot shattered through the air. She lost her balance, her body drifting off the side of the snowmobile. Letting go of the throttle, Graham swung his arm behind him to catch her. The mobile decelerated as the other mobile approached closer.

"Hang on!" Graham called.

Desperate for something to help him go faster, Layla pressed into him, squishing the black Lab, Emmy, between them.

More shots fired behind them. Her body flinched with each shot, but she didn't register any pain.

"Uh-oh," he muttered.

"Uh-oh? Worse than gunfire?"

Suddenly, the mobile launched off a raised strip of land and twisted in the air. Graham's hands struggled to maintain their grip on the steering wheel.

Layla braced for impact, trying to hold Emmy in place. The snowmobile struck the ground, slamming Layla's teeth together. Momentum spun the mobile into orange boundary tape, wrapping it around them. The mobile slowed, balancing on its right blade before pounding back into the packed snow.

Then all was silent...

Teresa Summers is an almost-native Colorado girl who loves the outdoor mountain life but leaves jumping off cliffs and skiing down the back slopes to her much more adventurous characters. When not writing her next romance, she is a music teacher and mom to four amazing kids who are also more adventurous than she is. *Secrets Beneath the Snow* is her first published work.

Books by Teresa Summers

Love Inspired Suspense

Secrets Beneath the Snow

Visit the Author Profile page at LoveInspired.com.

SECRETS BENEATH THE SNOW

TERESA SUMMERS

LOVE INSPIRED SUSPENSE
INSPIRATIONAL ROMANCE

 **LOVE INSPIRED® SUSPENSE**
INSPIRATIONAL ROMANCE

Recycling programs
for this product may
not exist in your area.

ISBN-13: 978-1-335-63865-6

Secrets Beneath the Snow

Love Inspired
22 Adelaide St. West, 41st Floor
Toronto, Ontario M5H 4E3, Canada
www.LoveInspired.com

Printed in Lithuania

MIX
Paper | Supporting
responsible forestry
FSC® C021394

For God hath not given us the spirit of fear;
but of power, and of love, and of a sound mind.
—*2 Timothy* 1:7

To my Heavenly Father, Who is my source of strength each and every day. And to Trevor, Nathan, Zachary, Seth and Adalynn. I love you!

ONE

Nothing was as cold as a tomb of snow. Even if Graham McAllister's tomb was man-made, on a well-maintained ski run on Silver Ridge Mountain, deep within the Colorado Rockies.

Its rugged peaks beckoned world-class skiers to its diamond runs from all over the world. The powder coated the mountain in undisturbed white, hanging heavy on the evergreens' branches. There was nothing like tipping over a ridge, skis sinking into the powder.

It was fresh. Pure. Just like a first kiss.

Unless it buried you beneath its force.

Which was why Graham always took his job on the ski patrol seriously. And why he agreed to crawl into a hole he could barely move in.

The freedom of the slopes called to Graham, even as he huddled in a hole he dug. Normally, he didn't mind training exercises. They prepared him and his avalanche-certified black Lab, Emmy, to find those taken within a wave of a snow. But normally he wasn't the one buried, waiting to be found.

Yet today, not one person volunteered. So here

he was, praying his fellow ski patrol hadn't forgotten him and punched out early to party on a Friday afternoon.

Memories of digging out victims from an avalanche two years ago rampaged his mind, their bodies mangled from the brute force of snow. He slammed his eyes closed against the image.

Where was his ski team? They should have been here by now.

He zipped and unzipped the collar of his patrol coat. Anything to keep from listening to the rhythm of his breath reverberating against the icy walls, accompanied by his pulse thumping in his ears.

Why did his nightmares have to bombard him now? Nightmares that had increased since Ollie's death three weeks ago.

No, not death. Murder.

He zipped faster, but the teeth caught on his neck. A growl escaped his throat, and he kicked his heel into the cavern's wall.

Where was Emmy?

He glanced at his watch. Twenty minutes. Ten more and, in real-world circumstances, his chance of survival would be cut in half.

Graham dropped his head back against the jagged wall of snow. The icy-blue cave surrounding him had dulled to gray. Outside, the coming storm must be settling around the mountain, darkening the midafternoon sky. He was running out of time.

He should have called in sick today. Or maybe not. Being in a hole was better than wallowing in his regrets at home with nothing to do. It only reminded him that never again would Ollie pound on his door after a heavy snow, ready to tackle the back slopes.

Home only reminded him he had lost a friend. Not just a friend—a brother.

"Come on, Emmy." His voice bounced off the frigid walls with a hollow echo.

He trusted Emmy. She was good at her job as a Colorado Rapid Avalanche Deployment, CRAD, certified Lab.

It was his patrol team he didn't trust. Or maybe it was just his patrol director.

Something about the guy triggered an inner alarm. How could he not want to investigate the circumstances surrounding Ollie's death? Ollie had been one of them.

Emmy was unsettled too. She always stood rigid, on alert, as if sensing something wrong on the ski patrol. Since Ollie had been Emmy's previous handler, her senses seemed to be on extra high alert now.

Another minute ticked by on his watch. Another minute to keep searching Anaconda Gulch before the coming storm hit, gone. It didn't matter that he had already scoured the area for hours over the last three weeks. Ollie's phone had to be buried there somewhere beneath the snow, close to where he had supposedly fallen off into the gulch.

According to the text Ollie had sent Graham immediately before he died, that phone contained pictures that would prove it was murder.

He owed it to Ollie to find his killer.

A muffled crunch of snow drifted down from the surface. Graham stiffened.

He released a slow breath as claws scratched up above Graham's den. Black paws broke through the barrier, followed by a long, wet nose sniffing into the hole.

Graham closed his eyes as Emmy's wet tongue slid across his cheek. The chuckle she always pulled out of him contrasted with his mood. "Yep, it's me, Emmy." He reached up and scratched her ears. "Twenty-two minutes. You made me wait twenty-two minutes."

With only half her body inside the hole, she shook her head, whipping one floppy black ear backward.

Graham reached up and flipped it back over. "What do you mean, it's not your fault?" Graham cupped her jaw in his hand. "It's because you miss Ollie, isn't it?"

Emmy stopped panting, her brown, almost copper, eyes meeting his.

Missing Ollie. Something they had in common.

"Don't worry, girl. I'll find out what happened to him. I promise."

As if in agreement, Emmy backed away from the hole to allow two patrol members to dig him out. Once his arm cleared the hole, Graham dangled Emmy's black rag, who grabbed it in her teeth and pulled.

Applause sounded from the spectators watching beyond the orange boundary rope. A group of college-age guys with bright colored coats and fur-trapper hats let out a couple of obnoxious hoots. Probably the same characters he had chased back across the boundary earlier.

Graham knelt, rewarding Emmy with a game of tug-of-war, but it lacked the same vigor as when she played with Ollie. Emmy pulled the rag free, then sat politely while Graham rubbed behind her ears.

When Ollie would do this, Emmy always hooked her front paw over his arm, as if to hold him close, and licked his hand. Something she had not yet done with anyone else. Including Graham.

Jim Simmons skied over, wearing the same red patrol coat with the white cross Graham wore.

He handed Graham his skis. "Emmy did great, again."

Graham straightened and took his skis. "Twenty-two minutes. She used to do it in fifteen."

"Well, she is seven years old. Besides, some of that time was Zane waiting for your scent to drift up from the snow."

Yeah, the guy probably would've waited until morning if not for the spectators watching the demonstration. Graham shot a look toward Zane, who was talking with another patroller. Their eyes locked.

The boss he could never please.

Graham returned his attention to Jim. "Emmy had faster times with Ollie."

"Man, you know Emmy is adjusting. It's only been three weeks. Give her a chance. Ollie may have been her handler, but she knows you almost as well. Shoot, she spent enough time with you."

Graham snapped his boots into his bindings. "That doesn't make me Ollie."

Jim patted Graham on the shoulder. "She'll adapt."

Graham wasn't so sure. Emmy still whimpered by his door to go home at night.

He looked down to call her over, but instead of sniffing around the snow or sitting ready for her next cue, she stood at the top of a snow berm, her body rigid, the fur on her neck raised.

Graham skied toward her. "What is it, girl?"

He followed Emmy's line of sight to someone in black snow gear. The skier blended in with the other spectators yet stood out.

The skier's hood shadowed his identity, along with a bulky scarf concealing the lower half of his face. Centered in his ski goggles' mirrored reflection stood Graham in his red patrol coat. The skier's gaze never wavered, even as a child next to him stumbled into his leg.

Graham's skin itched.

The crowd dispersed, but the guy didn't move. He stood motionless, keeping Graham framed in his ski goggles.

The hair on Graham's neck prickled. Why was

the guy so focused on him? And, more bothersome, why did the guy seem familiar?

Graham stared back, unable to move.

A hand gripped his arm. He jolted.

Zane Price, his patrol director, appeared next to him. "Graham, I thought I told you to stay clear of Anaconda Gulch."

Graham jerked his arm away. While trying to slow his accelerated heart rate, he searched the boundary for the stranger, but he had disappeared.

Graham inhaled to slow his breath back to normal. "What? No *Good job on the demonstration*? No comment on how Emmy did?"

Zane crossed his arms. "Bailey told me she saw you head over there. Again."

Graham scoffed. He shouldn't be surprised that Bailey had ratted him out. She was, after all, Zane's sister. Although, any member of his team would've done the same. None could be described as *loyal*. Except for maybe Jim.

It didn't really matter. He'd known life was a do-it-yourself project since he was ten. Since his mom had decided to break up their team of two by leaving him for her newest boyfriend.

Ollie had insisted that God was good and would never leave him. If only Graham could believe it.

He tugged at his gloves, digging his fingers deeper into their fleece lining. "It's for Ollie, Zane."

Zane didn't react. He never really reacted to anything. "It was an awful accident, and I'm sorry. I really am."

"If that were true, you could—"

"I am sorry, but you cannot be near Anaconda Gulch. The avalanche center said to stay clear of there. It's too unstable. Especially with this new storm approaching."

Graham fisted his hands. Even CAIC, the Colorado Avalanche Information Center, couldn't stop him from discovering how his friend had ended up dead. "They never found his cell phone, Zane. If I can find it, I know it will prove his death wasn't an accident. I don't understand why you aren't with me on this."

Graham looked to Jim to back him up, but his friend only shrugged.

Yeah, thanks, Jim. That was a lot of help.

Zane narrowed his eyes. "If there is a phone, you won't find it until the spring melt. Besides, the coroner's report said—"

"You think I care about the coroner's report? Yeah, he may have died by falling into the gulch, but Ollie was smart and an expert skier. What was he doing out there, anyway?"

Zane scratched his jaw with his glove. "Doesn't matter. You follow orders."

"Is that all you care about? One of our own died suspiciously, yet you aren't willing to ask questions?"

"Not when CAIC warns of avalanche danger. This isn't about Ollie. This is about safety. Steer clear, or you're off patrol."

Before Graham could argue, Zane skied off.

Jim patted Graham's back. "Bummer. I guess you have to stop poking around the gulch until spring."

Graham shrugged off Jim's hand. "Not going to happen."

"Hey, I believe you, man. I'd help, but I don't want to lose my job."

Graham slapped his helmet on and latched it under his chin. "Lifts close soon. I'm going to start clearing out the west runs."

With a low whistle, he signaled Emmy to his side before starting down Rambling Run, an easy green.

What he wouldn't give to dive into Slater's Bowl, sinking low into his skis with abandon. Clear his head.

Skiing to the west of the mountain with Emmy keeping pace at his side was per protocol, until the skier dressed in black caught his attention next to the boundary rope.

Graham locked eyes with the stranger's mirrored goggles. With a mock salute, the guy crossed beneath the rope and took off.

"Not on my watch," Graham muttered. "Come on, Emmy, let's go."

He skied past the boundary, then scooped up Emmy to perch on his shoulders. With a hard shove on his poles, he dipped down the hill. The guy picked up speed, leading deeper into unmarked terrain.

The skier veered around a crop of boulders. Graham rounded the same corner, but the stranger had disappeared.

Graham slowed, scanning the pines, their branches burdened with snow. The surrounding white rolled with unmarked softness. No evidence anyone else had been there.

Graham lowered Emmy to the ground. The air hung heavy, absorbing all other sounds. A bird's squawk echoed through the silence.

Graham's eyes followed the sound to the sky. No bird in sight. His gaze returned forward.

The skier materialized in front of him, and Graham's heart slammed into his rib cage.

He sucked in air, but he refused to budge. He wouldn't give in to this guy's twisted game.

Although, now that they were standing close, the guy looked more like a woman hidden under a bulky coat.

Emmy eyed the stranger, but her tail was wagging like she was meeting a new friend. Yeah, his dog might not be a lot of help if things got nasty. "You can't be over here."

The skier jerked their head toward Emmy. "I'm here for the dog."

Yep, a woman's voice filtered through the scarf. "Sure you are. For real, you can't be over here."

The stranger looked behind her, then to each side before she pulled down the scarf and dropped the hood. When she raised her goggles, blue-gray eyes, almost iridescent, stopped his breath. He stumbled backward.

It couldn't be, but he had memorized these eyes, stared into them. Eyes that haunted his memories.

Emmy bolted over to the woman, prancing around her.

After all this time, could it really be Layla?

He started to reach for her, an instinct, then pulled back, his chest tightening.

"Where have you been?" He didn't care how it sounded. Yeah, he was mad.

Even so, he had to grip his poles to keep from reaching out. She still had that effect on him.

She took a deep breath as she straightened to her full height. "I want my brother's dog back. Now."

Layla Quin should have never returned to Silver Ridge. Especially since it was Graham who stood between her Emmy. Now she had to convince him the only way she could keep going, to keep surviving, was if Emmy came along. And not tell him why.

Graham's hard stare penetrated through the falling flurries and made her queasy. "Get a rescue from wherever you disappeared to. You have no right to claim Emmy after disappearing for two full years."

Sure, she probably could adopt a dog, but it wouldn't be Emmy.

The dog she'd helped Ollie pick out of a litter of five. The puppy she and Ollie had taken turns walking every three hours throughout the night. The puppy she'd taught how to sit. The dog Ollie had trained to find people. The only dog she could trust.

Her dead brother's dog.

Layla's eyes shuttered closed. *Dead.* She still couldn't believe it.

"If you wanted Emmy, you should have talked with Ollie while he was alive."

Graham's words bruised deep. She reminded herself that he didn't know. Didn't know that she'd been running for her life. That she'd witnessed a murder, and now that murderer was after her. But still…

Graham's coat rustled as he crossed his arms, waiting for her to reply.

If she trusted anyone with Emmy, it would be Graham. In fact, she almost trusted him enough to tell him her story. After all, not so long ago, he'd believed her when no one else did.

But she couldn't.

The corrupt district attorney Cameron Flint would make Graham a target. Make it impossible for him to go home again.

She needed to stay focused, retrieve Emmy and then disappear to where Flint would never find her, the man who'd stop at nothing to hide the murder she'd seen him commit.

Graham pushed his ski goggles up onto his head. "You don't have anything to say for yourself?"

How could the man still render her speechless under the intensity of his gaze?

She closed her eyes, feeling the snowflakes

quickening on her cheeks. "I just want Emmy" was all she could force out beyond the lump swelling in her throat.

Maybe if she avoided looking at him, his toasted-brown eyes wouldn't trigger the gushing memories.

Memories of skiing with her brother and wearing cozy socks in front of the fireplace. Memories of not being afraid the wrong turn would leave her dead.

But the heaviest memories included this man, who still had endearing reddish-blond curls escaping from beneath his helmet, his thick reddish beard beckoning her fingers to touch.

Since age seventeen, her brother's best friend had been her friend and secret crush. Until just before she fled, when an undercurrent of something new began to stir between them.

She gave her head a shake. She was twenty-four now and struggling to survive. Time to give up childhood dreams.

Even so, his gaze penetrated to her core.

He saw her. Always had. And not just the piece of her that everyone saw, but the deep, vulnerable piece protected by the walls only he could break down.

So how could she demand Emmy when she teetered on the edge of running into his embrace, telling him everything?

Anyone but him would make this so much easier.

Emmy nuzzled her head beneath Layla's glove

as if Layla had been gone a week, not two years. Wow, how she'd missed this dog.

"Ollie said you went to school in Hawaii, but I thought you would have at least been here for his funeral."

Graham's tone made her flinch. Tears burned the backs of her eyes and caused ripples in her vision. Again.

Where was the Graham who'd held her when she cried? Where was the Graham who'd reassured her he would be there for her?

She stood up straighter. For the past two years, she'd held *herself* together; she could do it again.

Alone. Nothing had changed and nothing will.

"I don't like flying. I'm going to take Emmy with me now."

Too much time had already passed. The snow was falling faster, and it wouldn't take long for Flint to catch wind she was in town.

She dug deep into her coat pocket, past the can of Mace she always carried with her, to the treats she'd put in there for Emmy. She pulled one out and used it to entice the canine into coming with her as she skied away.

"I can't let you take Emmy."

She flinched but didn't stop—until something bolted out of the brush in front of her. Startling backward, Layla dropped both the treat and her poles to reach for her Mace.

A rabbit? Really?

Her heart thumped, its rhythm pulsing in her ears. She needed to get a grip.

Graham closed the distance between them, oblivious to the fact that her breath was stuck in her lungs. "I don't understand you, Layla. After everything Ollie did for you, how could you just abandon him like that?"

His words seeped into her belly and soured. Didn't Graham know her better than that? "Nobody loved my brother more than me."

Graham scoffed. "Really? So what's the real reason, then? Why couldn't you find time in your schedule to fly home for your brother's funeral?"

His accusations pummeled her already-fractured heart. She would've been there, but so would've Flint.

Instead, she had stood in her lonely hotel in Omaha, hugging her Bible and praying as the chills of loss ransacked her body. Oh, she hoped Ollie understood.

She needed to get out of here, out of Silver Ridge, before she collapsed into a puddle beneath Graham's words. She clawed for her poles in the snow. "Why do you care?"

He shifted his weight. "Ollie was my friend. He may have tried to avoid talking about you, but your departure was eating him alive. You couldn't have even called? What? You wanted to abolish all ties with the brother who gave up so much for you?"

No. He couldn't do this to her. Her hands clenched her ski poles until their rubber grip imprinted through her glove and into her palm. "It wasn't like that."

Graham came closer. "Then tell me, what was it like? Because all I see is a kid sister who walked away from the brother who loved her."

Rebellious tears traced down her cheeks, but she didn't look away. "You have no idea what you are talking about."

He crossed his arms over his chest. "Really? Because from where I sit, you left without ever saying goodbye."

"I said goodbye. To him."

"Really?"

"Yes, he's the one who told me to go."

"And you think that gives you an excuse to never contact him again?"

"I couldn't contact him."

"And why is that?"

"Because I didn't want him killed." The words punched out of her mouth before she could stop them.

Graham's arms went limp at his sides. His bearded jaw ridged.

"A lot of good that did me." A sob seized Layla's chest. She blew out a stream of air. "He died, anyway. In a silly accident."

Graham's eyes narrowed. "It wasn't an accident."

Layla wiped away a tear with her gloved finger. "What do you mean?"

"I'm saying that Ollie didn't die in an accident."

"I'm confused. The paper said—"

"The paper said only what it was allowed to say. I'm saying that Ollie never would've been by Anaconda Gulch if someone hadn't baited him there. Besides, Ollie was the best skier on patrol. He knew the gulch and understood that drifted snow over a cliff would give way if he skied over it. He wasn't stupid."

"You think someone—"

"I think someone killed Ollie and dumped his body over the cliff. I just don't know why."

Layla's pulse pounded louder than his words. "What?"

"There's more." Graham sighed, as if considering whether he should continue. After a few decisive breaths, he said, "The day he was killed, I received a text from him saying that he had some crazy important pictures to show me on his phone, but since the data service was in and out, they wouldn't send."

Layla's breath quickened, huffing in and out of her nose. No, this couldn't be happening.

"I tried to tell the authorities, but they have done nothing. I don't know what it's going to take to get someone to believe me." He paused and tilted his head. "Are you okay?"

Layla leaned into her poles, the world spinning. Her eyes scanned the forest. *He* had killed Ollie. Her brother's accident hadn't been an accident. After all this time, trying to protect her brother from the deranged DA by not calling, Cameron Flint had killed him, anyway.

No doubt to lure her out of hiding.

Every sound of the forest, every gust of breeze, carried with it the danger she had just put Graham in. How foolish could she be?

Regret softened the lines of his face. "I'm sorry. I shouldn't have sprung it on you like this. Do you need to sit down somewhere?"

Layla's breath came in gasps. "I should have never come."

"Now, I wouldn't say that. You're a little late, but—"

"No, you don't understand. He knows I'm here." Graham's brow lowered. "Who?"

Bile bubbled from her stomach and burned her throat. "I've put you in danger, Graham. I'm so, so sorry."

A high-pitched whine escaped from Emmy as she stared into the forest.

Graham moved closer. "Layla, tell me what's going on."

"I can't. I can't get you involved in this. It already got Ollie killed. I can't stand to lose you too."

"I'm already involved."

A growl rumbled from Emmy's throat, the hairs along her back coming to a ridge. Graham ignored Emmy.

Instead, he gripped Layla's shoulders. "What do you know, Layla? Tell me everything."

The truth dangled at the front of Layla's mouth, ready to break free for the first time in two years, but Emmy's bark stopped her.

Graham leaned over to grab Emmy's harness just before a bullet splintered a hole into the pine behind him.

Graham stiffened, his gaze scanning the forest. "Who in the world…"

Layla didn't have to ask questions. She knew who wanted her dead.

She grabbed Graham's sleeve and yelled, "Run!"

TWO

Graham's pulse ramped into a thunderous speed. A gunshot?

He moved in front of Layla as he canvassed the trees, trying to see beyond their snow-burdened pine needles. The white flakes from the sky quickened, falling fat and round.

A branch only a few paces away bounced, the snow shaken from its needles. Graham squinted, trying to glimpse their attacker, but the space was empty.

"What the—"

Again, a shot ricocheted through the air, but from ten degrees west. Was it the same shooter, or were there two? Emmy whined and pranced in a circle.

Layla yanked on his arm. "Graham, run!"

Her panic-choked voice matched her wide eyes. Then he understood.

This shooter wasn't after him. He was after Layla.

Everything shifted as an urge to protect her gathered in his chest. Why would someone shoot at Layla? It didn't matter. What mattered was getting her to safety.

Graham gathered Emmy onto his shoulders. "Go, go, go!" he shouted. They launched north, away from the shooter, with Layla in the lead. Graham followed behind in her tracks.

Emmy's weight pulled him to the left, but with one hand keeping her balanced, he leaned forward into his boots, pushing harder against the poles gathered in his other hand.

The icy wind stung his eyes, but he didn't take time to lower his eye gear. Not when a single second could give the gunman an advantage.

In front of him, Layla veered to the left, spraying snow as she went around a short crag. He followed, but the need to pick up the pace pounded in his head like a drum.

"Faster!"

Layla's arms pulsed like pistons against her poles, but they slowed as the energy drained away from her movements. Out-skiing the gunman wouldn't keep them alive. They needed to find a place to hide.

The ground leveled, removing downward momentum. They plowed their skis side to side against the powdery snow until they could shelter behind a boulder.

Their huffs resounded in the silence. Neither spoke. If the gunman was on skis, he could be right behind them, following the trail they left in the snow.

Graham inhaled through his nose, trying to slow down his breathing, but the pump of his heart pounded hard, even after he lowered Emmy to the ground.

Flakes now cascaded from the gray sky, creating a thick curtain that was impossible to see through. Graham strained to hear the swish of their pursuer's skis, but the snow insulated all noise. The gunman could be on the other side of the boulder, for all he knew, waiting.

Graham caught Layla's gaze and motioned for her to stay silent. Layla nodded with a brave tilt of her lips, but she let out a trembling sigh. Keeping his shoulder against the boulder, he shuffled around to the other side.

No one. At least, not from what he could see, which, with the falling snow, wasn't very far.

He came back beside Layla. "We may be in the clear."

Layla raised her goggles, her face in a tight grimace. "No, we aren't in the clear. I will never be in the clear. He is probably blocking our way back to the trail. In his mind, either the storm kills us or he will."

Graham flattened himself against the boulder. "Who? What is he after?"

Layla's grip on her poles shifted, as if she was preparing to take off again. She swallowed. "I can't get you involved—"

"I'm already involved, Layla."

"—or you'll end up like me. Never allowed to go home again."

Layla's voice pinched the word *again* into a

squeak. She looked like the seventeen-year-old who needed his understanding all over again. His support. But in one swift motion, she swiped the vulnerability from her features.

She straightened her shoulders. "I've been surviving on my own just fine. I'd rather do that than see anyone else get hurt."

A stab of appreciation for her strength warmed him. She was no longer a troubled teenager. No, she had grown into a woman. A woman whose beauty matched her strength.

He jerked his gaze forward. Lack of focus could get them killed. "Whether or not you meant to involve me, it's too late. I have to know what I'm fighting against."

She opened her mouth as if ready to argue, but a gust of snow blasted into them, ripping away her argument. "Fine. But first we need to find shelter."

Graham nodded. "We need to go back. We're too far off trail for me to know the way down the mountain. If we keep going, we'll be lost in the storm."

Layla shuddered as her breathing intensified. "No, we can't. If we backtrack, he'll be waiting to kill us."

"Getting lost in a blizzard means we're dead for sure. And I don't know about you, but freezing to death does not sound pleasant."

"Neither does being shot dead." Her gray-blue eyes flashed, sparking something deep inside him. "He's wanted me dead for two years. He'll stop at nothing—even killing my own brother to lure me out of hiding."

A chill coursed down Graham's limbs. Her gaze drilled into his without blinking. No tears. No hysterics. Just facts, as cold as the rock pressed against his back.

Why had she waited so long to come home? He could have helped her sooner. "What have you gotten yourself into?"

Layla's eyelids slid closed. "Please, Graham, I know you know this mountain well enough to survive. It's our only shot."

Graham ran a gloved hand over his beard, which was caked in ice. He had a compass with him. And a map. It was part of the gear he always carried with him in his patrol pack. But in a whiteout, it wouldn't be enough.

He scanned the area. He didn't recognize any of the formations, but he knew the direction where they'd left the trail.

He reached into his pack and pulled out a map. Snow drenched the crinkled parchment as he studied the trail they had left. He traced his finger along the direction they'd run.

According to this, if he was correct, they may have a chance.

"We have one shot." He tapped the map. "Lone Man's Hut. It's a backcountry ski shack up over that ridge. Ollie and I camped there a few times with Emmy."

He pointed to the west, but they could only see a few feet up.

Layla nodded and repositioned her goggles. "Okay, let's go."

Graham gripped her elbow. "Visibility will only get worse. We will be exposed to this storm's elements. We could pass the cabin within ten feet and not even know it."

Layla reached down and rubbed Emmy's head. "But we have Emmy."

The wind blew a gust of snow into Graham's face. They were wasting time discussing this. They needed to make a choice and go with it. He glanced behind them. He'd rather face a gunman than a whiteout without shelter. "Are you sure the gunman would wait for us out in this storm?"

Layla's eyes widened. "I think he will wait there until morning. And it's probably not just one. He has help." Her voice raised in pitch. "We can't go back to the trail, Graham. We'd be dead for sure."

Layla's pleading voice tugged on Graham's heart. He couldn't force her to go back to the trail. Besides, he might have a better chance with the storm than an army he couldn't see.

With a sigh, he lowered his goggles. "Stay close."

They took off, the falling snow pelting their coats. The ground inclined. With side-to-side motions, they made their way up the terrain. Their skis weren't meant to move uphill, and the motion challenged his muscles.

Emmy's legs sank into the snow, but at the slower pace, she hopped along beside them.

With the steep incline of the slope, it didn't take long before Graham's thighs were burning.

He brushed away the icicles hanging from his beard, but they came back within minutes. The ache in his lungs constricted his breath. He used his poles to pull himself, but Emmy was wearing down. She kept their pace, but her tongue dangled low, stopping every few hops to catch her breath.

The snow slanted horizontally, its sharpness striking his coat. His hands, even within his gloves, were numb. Emmy whimpered. If his toes, insulated inside his boots, were throbbing, he couldn't imagine how Emmy's paws felt.

White had descended on them, visibility zero. If they were going to survive, they needed to find shelter. Quick.

The blustering snow manipulated Layla's sense of direction. The weight of the frigid ice pressed against her coat, zapping the air from her lungs.

Her muscles quivered. She strained against the weakness with gritted teeth to keep from collapsing. If she did, it would mean freezing to death. She had to keep moving, had to keep up with Graham, or else be separated from him by a wall of white.

She focused on her skis; her arms as useless as noodles to hoist herself farther.

Just one more step. Then another.

Taking the next step, she slammed into Graham's

back. Momentum carried her backward. She waved her arms to counter the gravity. If she slid down the hill, Graham may never find her.

With a swift twist of his body, Graham caught her by the elbow and helped stabilize her balance.

"Are you okay?" he shouted above the wind.

Her throat pulled so tight she could only nod. What had she gotten them into? She'd made a stupid decision. Instead of taking the chance that Graham could sneak around Flint and his men, she may have killed not just herself, but Graham and Emmy as well.

She wanted to cry, to grieve the regretful choice she'd made, but even her tears remained frozen.

"Hey," Graham said, "look at me."

She tried, but she barely had the strength to hold her head straight.

"I know the cabin is close by. It has to be. Keep going. Okay?"

No, not okay. Her muscles had shriveled her body into a useless carcass. But she nodded, anyway.

Somehow he must have believed her nod, because he looked at his compass and pointed in the direction they needed to go.

Layla swallowed her whimper as he started forward, but Emmy leaped in front of him. With a low growl, she bit Graham's sleeve and pulled him in the other direction.

Graham yanked his arm away. "Stop, Emmy. We have to keep going."

He tried to move forward, but Emmy refused, tugging harder in the opposite direction.

Layla gathered the strength to call Emmy to her. Why was she acting like this? Emmy was loyal to a fault. The only reason she would counter orders was—

Emmy knew something they didn't.

A small seed of fight renewed within Layla. "We should follow her."

Graham pointed farther up the slope. "The compass says we need to go this way."

Layla looked up the slope, then back down at Emmy. No, Emmy wasn't wrong.

Layla had learned to rely on gut feelings over the last couple of years, and her gut said to follow Emmy. "I trust Emmy's instincts over your compass."

It was impossible to interpret Graham's reaction beneath the icicles hanging from his face, but she had the impression his feelings were almost hurt. "What if she's wrong?"

Layla raised her chin, gathering what remained of her energy. "What if you're wrong? Either way, we are taking a risk."

Graham looked at his compass, its arrow pointing true north. But if he was off on their starting position, they could walk right by the cabin without even knowing it in this kind of visibility.

Emmy whimpered again, her black fur nearly hidden beneath the snow clumping to it.

With a sigh, he put his compass into his pocket. "Okay, girl. We'll follow you."

Emmy bounded in the opposite direction.

Layla followed Emmy without hesitating. As she passed Graham, she heard him mutter, "I hope she's right."

White swirled around them, evaporating the surrounding trees. Emmy disappeared, then returned, making sure they were still following.

Layla's chest clenched off the airflow to her lungs. Had she done the right thing in trusting Emmy? It didn't matter. The decision had been made.

She didn't know how much time had passed, but just when she thought she would collapse, she saw a wood-planked wall that contrasted with the curtain of white.

Emmy sat in front of the wall, panting. Almost gloating. Layla would have laughed if she had the strength.

Graham moved past her to Emmy and rubbed the dog's head. "Good girl."

Once Graham shoved open the door, they all tumbled into the cabin, carrying their skis. A torrent of snow drifted through the threshold as both Graham and Layla rammed their shoulders into the door to shut it. It finally closed.

Layla slid down to the floor, gathering air into her burning lungs, her eyes closed. She was too tired to sob, even though relief had crashed into her with a powerful punch.

The nylon of Graham's ski pants swished as he, too, slid to the floor. Forcing her eyelids open, she glanced at him. He leaned his head against the door. Between breaths, he said, "Never again. That was stupid."

"I'm sorry."

"Well…" He inhaled to control his breathing. "Just…"

Words didn't come to him, but he reached over and squeezed her arm.

His touch flooded warmth through the chill, reaching deeper than skin level. She had been alone for so long. But she couldn't let him in. Look how she'd almost gotten him killed in such a brief time.

If she cared about him, she could not allow her need for an ally to be his demise.

She pulled her eyes away from him, away from the face she had always loved looking at, to take in their shelter.

The cabin didn't have much; Graham was right to call it a *shack*. It looked like something a trapper had built at the turn of the century. In fact, it might be a leftover from a trapper. But at least it held against the moaning wind. Not having any windows made that easier, even if Layla longed to see outside.

The one room contained only two bare green cots on either side of an antique cast-iron stove. Without even a kitchen, cooking would have to be Old West–style. At least a sizable stack of firewood stood in the corner.

The other corner on the left side of the door was a closet, the only part of the cabin that had been tweaked since at least the 1920s. Even that looked crudely built, with misaligned planks of wood.

But it was shelter.

A whimper from Emmy grabbed Layla's attention.

Emmy stumbled like she wanted to lie down but forced herself back up. Her skin shook beneath the snow caked into her fur. Her tail hung low as she panted heavily.

Layla pulled her gloves off her stiff hands and forced herself up on trembling legs. It didn't matter how tired she was. Emmy needed her.

Graham also set into action and headed to the cast-iron stove. Shivering, Layla staggered to the closet.

The closet held extra skis, poles, a shovel, avalanche probes, a medical kit and even a tool kit, but no blankets. A cabin meant for backcountry skiers had to have blankets somewhere.

Next to one cot, she spotted a large brown tote that almost blended into the wall. She scrambled over to it and lifted the lid.

The open tote reeked of body odor mixed with stale smoke. Three blankets had been shoved on top of two sleeping bags.

Layla pulled out all three and knelt in front of the stove, where Graham was working, loading it with firewood.

Layla pulled Emmy to her own body as she unbuckled the canine's red vest and harness. Then Layla wrapped the blanket around Emmy. Once the first blanket became saturated, Layla tossed it aside for a dry one, rubbing Emmy from her torso down to her legs.

Emmy's skin twitched beneath her touch, another whimper escaping her throat.

The second blanket also became soaked. Wrapping the last blanket around Emmy, Layla pulled the shivering dog close to her chest.

At the sound of crackling from the stove, Layla's shoulders caved forward around Emmy. "It's okay, girl. We're going to be okay."

Melted tears trickled down Layla's cheeks.

She couldn't break down now. Not when they were going to survive. Well, survive the night, at least. With a killer on her tail, the next day was never a guarantee.

As the fire glowed brighter and the kindling crackled, Emmy relaxed in Layla's arms, trembling.

Graham sat next to her. He had shed his red ski patrol coat and beanie. His forest green sweatshirt brought out his toasted brown eyes.

Layla resisted sweeping a lock that fell in front of his forehead back behind his ear. The gesture would probably weird him out, coming from Ollie's kid sister. Even if she'd never thought of him simply as her brother's best friend.

No. In fact, when loneliness nearly crumpled her need to survive, hiding in some cheap motel, she would think of Graham and fall asleep, dreaming up her own happily ever after.

But those were just dreams. This was reality. And in this reality, she'd almost killed him.

Sometimes, it would be so much easier to stop running.

No, she couldn't let her thoughts go there. She had to believe her running had purpose. That it would end.

Someday.

For now, her focus should be on taking as few people as possible down her bottomless rabbit hole.

Graham stroked his fingers up the bridge of Emmy's nose. "You did it, girl. You can rest now."

Emmy lay down, and Layla tucked the blanket tighter around the dog's body. "This is all my fault."

Graham's mouth pulled taut, like he wanted to agree with her but didn't want to say the words. "We'll be okay now."

Layla slid out of her coat and added it on top of Emmy. "For now. I should have never come back."

Graham settled next to her with one knee propped up, resting his arm across it. "About that. Are you going to tell me about where you have been? The truth?"

Once upon a time—in what felt like another lifetime—Layla had revealed to Graham the truth about why she'd left Denver for Silver Ridge to live with her brother four years older than her.

Back then, no one believed her story. Not her

parents. Not the cops. Not the shop owner accusing her of shoplifting.

She should've known that Cloe Barnes was too popular to want to spend time with her, but when the girl asked to meet her at the Sixteenth Street Mall, Layla thought for sure she'd made it into the "in" crowd.

Instead, the girl had planted a stolen necklace in Layla's pocket and let her take the rap for it.

To this day, she didn't know if Cloe had really intended to steal the necklace or if it was simply a twisted prank.

Whatever the case, Layla was the one who'd been arrested.

Her parents had said they believed her—but if so, why would they pack her up and send her to live with her brother? It was like she'd brought shame to their suburban illusion.

It didn't matter if they said they simply wanted her away from city life and bad influences. Truth was, they never believed her.

Not really. No one did.

Except for Graham.

Would he believe her now?

The corners of his eyes crinkled as his gaze intensified. "Tell me. Who's after you?"

Layla's eyes slid closed. She swallowed. "Cameron Flint."

Her heart dropped as shock rolled over Graham's face.

Well, maybe he wouldn't believe her after all.

THREE

Heaviness settled in Graham's stomach. He couldn't have heard right. Snow must have plugged up his ears.

A torrent of wind gushed against the cabin walls, sounding more like sand than snow.

Graham shook his head to clear the shock away. "Cameron Flint?"

Layla nodded, her fingers weaving deeper into Emmy's wet fur.

"You mean Cameron Flint, the district attorney? The guy they're already saying will be a senator in a few short years?"

Layla stilled, not meeting his eyes. She was retreating. It shouldn't hurt that she didn't trust him, yet it did. She had trusted him before. Why not now?

He leaned over to make eye contact. "Layla, tell me what happened. I'll believe you. I always have."

There, her head lifted, but vulnerability pinched her brow, like she didn't know if she should continue. "You said it yourself. The world believes he'll be a senator."

Graham smirked. "But I've heard stories about the guy. Trust me, he ain't perfect."

The corner of her mouth twitched like she wanted to smile, but it fell flat. She hesitated, then shifted her body. "Do you remember when I had just gotten the job as an event planner for the town?"

Oh, did he. She had met him and Ollie at the end of their shift, glowing. Radiant, was more like it. That was when he realized his feelings for her might be changing.

Then she'd disappeared.

He licked his lips. "Yeah, I remember. You were determined to prove yourself."

She shrugged. "They were giving me a chance. I didn't want to blow it. Anyway, I was staying late at the event center, getting ready for the fall festival. You remember, the one where kids come in costumes and paint pumpkins? Caramel-apple bar?"

Graham's stomach growled. "Please leave food out of this."

Again, her mouth twitched. If only he could make her smile break free.

She let out a shuddering sigh, as if unsure she wanted to go on. He inched closer. Just enough to reassure her he was on her side.

Her eyes closed. "It was after midnight, and I was taking out some trash behind the center when I heard an argument. I'd stepped into the alley, and there were gunshots. I looked up and stared into the eyes of Cameron, who was holding a gun with smoke swirling from the barrel. Someone lay on the ground in front of him, dead."

Graham blinked. "Murder? Why?"

She ran her hand down Emmy's ears. "I heard the word *embezzlement* from the dead man before the shot. That's all I know. Then Cameron told another guy with him to clean up the mess."

Graham's pulse thundered in his veins. Was this for real? "Someone else was there?"

She bit her lip and nodded.

If not for the snow pelting the cabin with hurricane-like winds, Graham would blaze down the mountain and into Flint's office, demanding answers. He'd known something was off about the guy.

A suit lording their authority to hide a crime was wrong. Twisted.

He didn't know if the heat flooding into his neck came from the stove warming the space or the rage burning in his gut.

Graham jumped to his feet and crammed his fingers through his hair. His eyes flitted from the wooden door, barely strong enough to keep the blizzard outside, to the cast-iron stove, a relic that probably hadn't been cleaned in years.

He needed to punch something. Or kick something. That would work too. But the doe-like eyes following his movements made him pause.

Layla huddled into Emmy, her face ashen against the dog's thick black coat. Emmy's ears pricked forward, more curious than scared. Confusion furrowed Layla's brow, but her lips tightened, like she refused to release any more of her secrets.

Graham raised his face to the ceiling, releasing a slow breath. Okay, he could be rational if he put his mind to it.

"Are you sure it was Flint?"

Her eyelids drooped. "You don't believe me."

Graham pinched the bridge of his nose. He knew Layla well enough to know the root of her statement. He should kick himself for even saying it. "That's not what I meant."

"I wouldn't lie. I don't lie."

"I know. Really. I just wondered, is there any chance you could've mistaken him for the murderer? It was dark."

Layla's fingers paused trailing over the top of Emmy's head. "I stared into his eyes. I heard his voice. I knew his voice."

"How?"

With a sigh, she wrapped her arms around her knees. "Because at the time, I was dating him."

And there it was again—the raw impulse to beat the guy.

She scoffed. "Don't look so shocked that a guy like him would be interested in someone like me. He didn't even know I had been arrested for theft. If the cops didn't believe that I didn't do it, Cameron Flint certainly wouldn't have either. So I never told him."

He ran a hand over his face. "Layla, that's not what I was thinking." Far from it. His thoughts were closer to why a guy like Cameron Flint got a chance with her when Graham never did. Or rather, another decent guy like him. She *was* his best friend's sister.

"It's okay," she interrupted his thoughts softly. "I know the whole thing is hard to believe."

Graham averted his gaze. "Okay. So you knew him. What about the other guy? Know who he was?"

"No. He was wearing a ski mask and hid in the shadows." Her voice was barely above a whisper. Ghostlike. "The only hint I have is that Flint told him to dispose of the body in the usual spot before hitting the lifts for his patrol shift."

Graham's pulse stuttered. "Patrol shift? As in ski patrol?"

"That's what I assumed. I told Ollie, but last I talked with him, he hadn't figured out who yet. The guy is a ghost."

And just like that, icy fingers tickled Graham's spine, lowering his body temp once again.

He shivered. Could he be working with a murderer and not know it? Well, more like an accomplice, but still.

Faces of his teammates flashed in his mind. Sure, he didn't always trust them, but murder? He couldn't believe it about any of them.

"What did he mean by 'the usual spot'?"

She shook her head, slowly, as if it weighed heavy. "I don't know."

Graham's mind churned. If they could find that

spot, they may have evidence to put Flint away. "What else do you remember?"

Layla rubbed her temples. "It was so long ago."

Graham's ski pants swished as he went to sit next to her again. He reached for her hand, pulling it from her temple to tuck between his palms. "Tell me what happened next, after he saw you."

She closed her eyes. "He said, 'What have you done, Layla? Now I have to kill you.' He raised his gun toward me. I shoved over the trash barrels before I ran around the corner of the building. I made my way along the river. I thought he might find me if I ran into town."

"So, he chased you?"

"He sent his sidekick after me." She stared at the planked floor, lost in the memory of her nightmare. The wood in the oven popped, and her body jolted.

Graham ran his thumb over her hand. "How did you get away?"

"I hid on a rock beneath a bridge."

Graham squinted, trying to remember what rock she was talking about.

"I found it when I first came to live with Ollie. It was my secret spot back when I didn't want to be found. It worked to escape Cameron too. I saw a truck drive by slowly. At one point, the truck stopped on the bridge. I thought he found me, but then he moved on, much slower than the speed limit."

"Did you see the truck?"

She nodded. "I peeked as it drove by. It was a

blue Chevy Silverado with a crunched right fender. Like he backed into a tree."

Graham blinked. He knew that truck's description. "You said a blue Silverado with a smashed right fender?"

A license number rolled off her lips in a whisper. "I memorized its plate."

Graham dropped Layla's hand and combed his fingers into his hair. "No way."

Yeah, he may have said he suspected Zane of something off-handed, but an accomplice to murder?

"What is it?"

Graham pressed his palms into his eyes. "That's the ski director's truck."

Her jaw dropped open. "You think it was him?"

What else could he do but shrug? Could Zane really do something like that when he worked so hard to help the injured on the slopes? It was almost like each injured person was someone he cared about. But who else had that exact truck?

He stood again, renewed energy making his legs restless. What should he do? He couldn't very well smash into headquarters and accuse the guy. Not if Graham didn't want to be perceived as the one in the wrong.

There was only one thing they could do.

He stilled and looked at Layla. Her eyes always reminded him of a fawn: vulnerable yet determined. Innocent, even when darkness seemed to chase after her.

She didn't deserve this. She didn't deserve to be wrongly accused of theft at seventeen, just like she didn't deserve to be on the run from a power-hungry murderer.

An urge to shut her in a closet while he figured this out came over him. Anything to protect her. And not just because it was what Ollie would want.

Even so, hiding was temporary. He would have to let her out eventually. The only way to get her out of this situation was to remove the threat.

The only way to remove the threat—at least, the only way he could think of—was to face it. Boy, he hoped he wasn't making the wrong decision.

He lifted his hand, hesitated, then pushed his hair out of his face. "Layla, you have to tell some-one about this."

Layla should've never told Graham her story. Not when he now wanted her to do the very thing she couldn't do.

"Don't say that." Her words came out low, sullen.

"But, Layla, Flint needs to be brought to justice. Who knows if he will kill again—or has already killed others?"

Layla gripped the blanket lying across Emmy, her knuckles turning white. "And I will be one of them if I even peek into Silver Ridge."

Graham's gaze scanned the ceiling, as if he could see the answer written there. If only it were that easy.

"Running is my only solution." She shut her

mouth before an offer for him to go with her slipped out.

Whoa. Where did that thought come from? Yes, she was lonely, but really...

Graham crossed his arms and paced. "You can't keep this to yourself, Layla. Look, I will go with you. You have me on your side."

"I had Ollie on my side, and look what happened to him."

He had no answers. No words. Ollie was dead.

Layla wobbled as she stood. Emmy came alert, her ears perked, focused on Layla's movement as if ready to come to her aid if needed. Layla found her balance and stepped toward him with her arms wrapped tightly around herself.

"Flint is powerful. He is a DA, for crying out loud. Who would ever believe me over him?"

"But he can't just get away with it." Graham's voice rose with intensity.

Layla would not back down. "So where does that leave me, Graham? The sacrifice for justice? He's a DA. Justice is on his side. Flint won't ever pay for anything. He'll just cut down anyone who gets in his way. That includes you."

"But running isn't the answer, either, Layla. What are you going to do, run forever? Alone?"

Layla forced a pathetic smile. "That's why I need Emmy. So I'm not alone."

Graham smoothed his hand over his beard. The wind beat against the shack's walls, the only sound between them as they stared at each other.

After several moments, Graham dropped his hand. "What if you talk to someone I know at the sheriff station, nothing official? Just to get his advice. Someone I think I trust, and I don't trust easily."

The muscle in his jaw ticked. She knew he didn't trust easily. She'd always guessed it stemmed from his mom leaving him, although she'd never known the full story.

Still she started to shake her head, but Graham reached out and cupped her cheeks in his hands.

"You are in danger now, Layla. What will change if you talk to this sheriff and then run? Why not take the chance for freedom?"

Her heart pounded in her chest. He couldn't ask this of her. "It's hard enough to be on the run from Flint without the authorities putting out an alert for a girl who falsely accused a bigwig."

"That won't happen."

"How do you know? Flint is not below lying about me. He'll get the cops after me too."

Graham's hands slid from her face to her shoulders. "Both running and telling someone your story is risky. Both are hard. You must choose which one is worth it. You must ask yourself *What if?*"

Layla's breath stuttered at that single question. What if? What if she could find a way home?

"I know you don't think they would believe you, but what if they do? What if you could be free?"

Graham's point resonated with hope in her chest. Hope she had difficulty snuffing out. What if she slipped over to the outskirts of Silver Ridge and spoke with his contact at the sheriff station?

What if they believed her?

No, they wouldn't. No one would believe her over a DA. Yet, a part of her wanted to try.

Layla stepped backward and shook her head. This was dangerous. Hope was dangerous.

She inhaled sharply and turned around. Without windows in the cabin, it was impossible to see the storm raging around them. She could hear the wind, but the snow could completely cover the cabin and she would never even know.

Her breath came in gasps, torn between what she knew and what she wished for. Her eyes twitched from one wall to the other.

She couldn't see.

She couldn't see out of this room. She couldn't see what one choice might bring over another.

"Layla?"

The four walls closed off her airway.

What should she do?

"Layla."

Graham's voice reached into her building panic. She needed that. A voice of reason. "I don't know what to do, Graham. It feels like anything I do could lead to death. I could trust, but trust the wrong person. I could run, but run to the place they would find me."

Graham's throat bobbed as he swallowed. "Running isn't any way to live, Layla. I promise I will protect you."

The irony brought a smirk to Layla's mouth. "That is what Ollie said on our last phone call a year ago. When he tried to bring me home."

A shadow cast over Graham's eyes. He understood the danger of trying to protect her, but, for some reason, he didn't turn away.

Instead, he raised his chin, his decision clear. "Ollie and I are different. Emmy can attest to that. Had it been me, I never would have told you to run."

Except Ollie knew no one would believe her. He'd heard her parents' grief when they thought their daughter had committed a crime.

Graham reached out and flipped her dark, dyed hair over her shoulder. "We can talk more tomorrow. We really should get some rest."

Yeah, maybe. Her brain hurt. Her body hurt. Yet falling asleep meant morning would come quicker, bringing with it hard choices. She'd have to face her fate.

Tonight, for one night only, the storm shielded her. In this shack, she was safe with Graham. The man she trusted more than anyone else.

Graham motioned to the cot as he opened the stove's door to stoke the flames. "I'll stay up minding the stove. You get your sleep."

Layla walked toward the cot, her frosted toes coming back to life with a burning sensation, but she only stood staring at it.

"Here." Graham lifted a sleeping bag out of the tote and laid it on the cot for her. "It's a little raunchy, but it'll keep you warm. The best this grand hotel has to offer."

It had been so long since someone had taken care of her. Helped her. She couldn't help but smile. "Thank you."

Graham studied her. His movements stalled. The corner of his mouth tilted up, but he jerked and turned his attention back to the sleeping bag.

When he finished, he straightened. "It's nice to see you smile."

Her cheeks warmed. He was simply being nice. Still, the way he glanced back at her almost seemed, well, somehow shy.

"There." He smacked his hands together as if proud of a job well done. "I shall leave you to get your sleep."

He stepped back to the stove.

With another smile tugging at her lips, she slid into the sleeping bag, ignoring its stench of sweat. She took a deep, calming breath, even the foul smell not overpowering the sprout of hope.

"Really, Graham, thank you for everything."

He reached for a log and rotated it in his hands. "Sure. It's what Ollie would have wanted."

Of course. For Ollie.

She should have expected that. After all, who would brave a storm, nearly losing his life, simply for her? No, his motivation was protecting Ollie's baby sister.

Rolling onto her side, she tried to get comfortable. The cot shifted as Emmy stepped up next to her and curled up against the backs of her legs.

Despite her desire not to face the morning, the added warmth lulled Layla asleep.

Until a thud hitting the wall awakened her.

FOUR

Graham had watched the dawn, his head churning about what he'd learned from Layla. It could be passed off as a conspiracy theory, something she'd made up to look like a victim—but in his gut, he knew it was true.

He reentered the cabin, arms loaded with firewood, the sun fully above the horizon now. Emmy released a little groan as she pranced over to him.

"Morning, girl." He reached down to scratch behind her ear, but Emmy pulled away, releasing a high-pitched whine.

He halted. Something seemed different. Off.

He glanced around, but everything remained as he'd left it.

He piled the wood next to the stove. Brushing away the wood residue from his hands, he moved toward Layla's cot.

The sleeping bag was bunched in a peculiar shape. He squinted. "Layla?"

He inched closer, careful not to awaken her.

No movement. Not even the rise and fall of her breath.

"Layla?"

He reached down to find her shoulder, but his hand sank into the nylon of the sleeping bag.

His heart lurched. Gritting his teeth, he whisked the sleeping bag off the bed.

Layla was gone.

Fighting off nausea, his gaze flitted around the room.

Where would she have gone? If she'd left on her own, her chance for survival shrank to almost nothing.

A scratching sound halted his circling thoughts. Emmy stood at the door, her fur ridging along her back.

No, Layla would never leave Emmy behind.

A muffled cry sounded from the other side of the wall. Graham spun toward it, but silence returned.

A sour taste filled his mouth.

Without a sound, Graham reached for the shovel he'd left by the door earlier. Emmy scratched at the door again, but he stopped her with his hand on her head.

A blast of cold air smacked his face as he opened the door. To his right, a small set of footprints led around the corner.

He motioned for Emmy to stay. No matter what, he couldn't let her get hurt. If she did, she couldn't do her job of rescuing people.

With a defiant sneeze, she lay down, slightly raised on her haunches.

Graham motioned harder. "No, you are not a combat dog." With a grunt, Emmy lowered all the way.

After a moment to make sure Emmy stayed, he followed the footprints.

Before rounding the corner, he pressed his back against the wall, listening.

Nothing.

Holding his breath, he tightened his grip on the shovel over his shoulder and spun around the corner.

His pulse throbbed in his neck. The disturbed snow showed a struggle, but no Layla. Only two sets of prints leading away from the cabin. One set looked half-dragged.

He blinked hard, forcing away his racing thoughts. Accusing thoughts that he'd failed her already.

No, Layla needed him focused. Clearheaded. Prepared for whatever these tracks led to.

Emmy peeked around the other corner. Graham rolled his eyes.

He held up his hand for her to stay again, hoping the dog would listen this time.

She groaned but lay down again.

Graham shifted his hands around the shovel and continued. The footprints led to a crop of boulders between two trees, then ended.

Graham inched forward, his heart pounding in his chest as he tried to quiet the crunch of his steps in the snow.

A man swung into the open with Layla pinned against his chest. Graham's muscles jolted.

Layla shrieked behind her captor's bare hand gripping her mouth.

Graham moved forward but stopped at the click of the gun held to her head.

"Don't come any farther," the man growled.

Graham swung his arms wide, the shovel dangling in his left hand. "Let her go."

The man adjusted the gun in his hand. "Don't move. If you do, she's gone."

Graham sucked in a breath. If the man fidgeted any more, he'd shoot without even intending to.

He backed up a step, trying to appear like less of a threat. *Come on, Graham. Think.* "You don't want to do this."

The man scoffed. "Oh, yeah? Why not? My boss needs to have a chat with her."

Which meant the man had orders not to kill her. At least, not yet. That played in her favor.

Graham glanced down at Layla. Tears flowed from her bloodshot eyes, making heat surge through his veins. He swallowed to control his temper. "Your boss could ask nicely."

The man's feet shifted. "Trust me, you want to stay out of this."

Before a question could form on Graham's lips, a flash of black fur launched at the gunman, gripping his sleeve in her jaws.

The man recoiled, loosening his grip enough for Layla to slip out of his grasp.

Before the man could recover, Graham charged, the shovel held forward like a javelin. The shovel speared the man's gut, knocking him off his feet. The man positioned his gun, preparing to shoot, but Graham whacked the shovel against the man's head full force.

The gun slipped from the man's hand as he fell into the snow, unconscious.

Layla gasped for breath, collapsing against a nearby tree while Emmy the rescuer pawed at her leg.

Graham stared at the body before he bent down and grabbed the gun. It weighed heavy in his hand.

The scene replayed in his mind. It could've ended differently. Ending with Layla or himself dead. Maybe he'd underestimated the danger Layla was in.

He aimed the gun at the man. Just in case. His throat tight.

If the purple blooming on the side of the man's head was any indication, he wouldn't be getting up for a while. Still, they couldn't be sure.

He glanced toward Layla. "You okay?"

She raised her chin, as if to prove she was made of tougher stuff than she appeared, but he saw the tremble in her jaw.

He nodded. "I saw some rope in that closet in the cabin. Can you grab it?" He turned back to the man at his feet, holding the gun steady.

Without a word, she ran toward the cabin. It

didn't take long before she returned with the coil of rope.

He handed her the gun while he tied up the man's ankles and wrists. When finished, he picked up the shovel and exchanged it for the gun. "Carry this while I drag him back to the cabin."

After shoving the gun into his waistband, Graham looped his hands under the man's arms and dragged him inside the cabin. He shoved him into the closet and blocked the door with a cot for added measure.

Not perfect, but it should hold the man long enough for them to get away. "We need to get out of here. Another one of Flint's cronies could be close behind."

Layla stared at the closet door and nodded. Her face clenched into tight lines as he could almost see the magnitude of her ordeal washing over her.

Not knowing what else to do, he took the shovel from her hand and leaned it against the cabin door. It slid to the floor with a clatter.

Layla didn't even flinch.

She opened, then closed her mouth. After a long exhale, she shrugged. "I hardly know how it happened. I heard a thud, and when I saw you gone, I thought something happened to you, so I went to look."

"It's over now. We need to get out of here before he wakes up."

But she didn't move. "He grabbed me from behind before I even saw him."

Graham turned her toward him. "But you survived."

Still, her shoulders quivered.

Graham's jaw tightened. He ached to take away her fear. But as much as he wanted to stand here and make promises about keeping her safe, they didn't have time. "We'll figure this out, but not here."

Her face changed, almost like a veil had lowered, hiding her thoughts. "Let's go."

Unease tingled down his back. Why did he have a feeling her mind was concocting a plan he wouldn't like?

He'd have to ask later. Now they needed to hurry.

While Layla tugged on her coat, he turned to the bucket of water by the door and snuffed out the fire before he donned his rescue pack.

Layla hurried to the door, Emmy at her heels as if trying to hurry them along.

Picking up his helmet, he hesitated. "Wait."

She came to him, her gray eyes searching his. He swallowed, then reached over and placed his helmet over her dark hair and buckled the chinstrap, trying to ignore the softness of her cheek as he did.

She tried to shrug away. "This is your helmet, Graham."

"Yep."

"Don't you need it?"

He tapped the helmet, then picked up his gloves. "I'm a much better skier than you."

She rolled her eyes. "Oh, the ego."

"Ready?" Graham tightened his pack's chest strap.

Layla's gaze flitted to his, strong and determined. "Ready."

Wow, he admired her grit.

They stepped into the sunshine, and Graham lowered his ski goggles against the brilliant reflection of the white landscape.

"That's not the way down, is it?" Layla's voice cut through the stillness. The tremble in her voice matched the tremble in her pointing finger.

Deadman's Bowl. Appropriately named after several inexperienced skiers had gotten in over their heads. Its drop-off into the fresh powder was only a few feet away.

The reason the shack was popular to backcountry skiers, including himself and Ollie. It was a rush.

"I know you gave me your helmet and all, but I don't think I can make it down that."

Graham set his skis down and stepped into the bindings. "This is the fastest way down the mountain."

Layla leaned to peek over its edge. She caught her breath and scrambled back toward the shack. "I can't do that!"

Graham motioned toward the cabin. "That man in the closet could wake up at any minute."

"The point is to stay alive. This drop-off is practically vertical. Besides, you tied him up."

"But another might be on his way." They needed off this mountain. Fast.

Graham examined Layla. Beads of sweat formed along her forehead. Yeah, maybe she wasn't quite ready for the bowl.

He turned to look toward the trail. It curved through the forest with less incline, but if they hurried, maybe they could make it before Flint's man escaped.

He flashed her a grin. Anything to ease the wrinkles in her brow. "Fine. We'll take the novice way down."

She wasn't a novice. He only wanted to tease her.

He was rewarded with a slight quirk of her mouth before she turned to face the trail. "I'm not going to dignify that with a response."

In any other circumstance, Graham would've chuckled. Instead, he skied toward the trail he knew lay buried beneath the snow south of the cabin.

He plowed down the trail, Emmy keeping pace at his side. Layla followed close behind. But urgency wouldn't leave him alone. They were too slow. At this pace, one of Flint's men could easily catch up.

He turned his head to tell her to go faster, but stopped cold. Above them, a snow-loaded ridge hovered, ready to break free.

Prickles traveled down the back of his neck like a thousand needles rendering him motionless.

The edge wanted to give way. He could feel it. All it would take was a vibration and the cornice would crumble, burying them in its fury.

He held his breath. This had been the route they'd

taken to the cabin last night. Clueless of the danger above their heads.

"Turn around." His voice hovered only one step above a whisper. "We can't continue beneath that."

Layla faced the cornice, clutching her poles. "But what other way down is there?"

Graham swallowed, his teasing from moments ago settling into his stomach like hot lead. She could make it if he helped her, right? She had to.

"There's only one other way off this mountain. And it is safer than causing an avalanche. Especially after last night's accumulation."

Layla squeezed her eyes closed, as if helpless to stop the truth from gushing out of Graham's mouth. She gave a little shake of her head.

If only there was another way. "We have to go back up. Back to Deadman's Bowl."

Layla ought to be used to this by now. Staring death in the face. She shuddered. If a crazed, powerful man didn't gun her down, a giant cliff of doom might be her undoing.

Her head spun as she gazed down a hundred feet below. Graham stood beside her, giving directions, something about leaning forward into her skis, but his words blurred together.

How had she gotten into this situation? Somehow, one decision after another had led her to danger's door. That was the problem—her decisions.

How could every decision she made only land her in deeper trouble?

And now, staring into the abyss of white below her, one wrong move would, at best, send her to the emergency room, where Flint would find her for sure. At worst, well…she forced that thought away.

Graham's hand gripped her arm. "Layla, are you listening?"

She gulped, tasting bile in the back of her throat. "I can't do this. I'm going to screw up. I know I am."

"No, it will be fine. I'm here to help you."

"I'm going to screw up because that is all I do. I screw up. No matter what I try to do, I end up making a bigger mess."

"Layla, that isn't true."

The inside of Layla's goggles began to fog up. "Yes, it is."

"Layla—"

"You can't deny it, Graham. Look at my life. I can't even go home. I can't make a single move without making matters worse. I shouldn't have ever returned for Emmy."

Graham rubbed her arm. "I'm glad you did. Now I know what is going on, and I can help."

"See, that's just it. You getting involved means you getting hurt. Another mistake."

His hands slid around her helmet as he dipped to look her in the eyes. "You can't know that. What if God brought you back so that I could help you?"

Layla sighed, shuddering. "Your life was simple yesterday morning before I showed up."

Graham smoothed his gloved thumb over her cheek. "Simple, yes, but also lonely."

Layla's heart stalled as she stared into his eyes, her words falling to pieces at her feet. Nothing would ever be the same after her choice to come back to Silver Ridge. She wanted to believe that the ray of hope Graham cast meant something, but she knew that hope would shatter. Somehow.

A rustling followed by a moan within the cabin shattered the silence. Layla's heart rate jumped. The man was waking up.

Graham must've heard it too. He straightened. "Layla, listen to me. We have to get down this mountain. I need you to trust me."

Layla could only nod. How tight had he tied the rope? Would the man be able to escape quickly?

Graham turned her face toward him again. "Listen carefully." He leaned forward into his boots. "Always lean forward. Even if you feel like you are going too fast." His words picked up speed. "People have an instinct to lean back when they get scared, but if you do that, you'll lose your balance. Feet must be centered below the hips and shoulders. Ski aggressive."

Layla gave a weak nod.

"Keep your knees loosely bent."

She nodded again.

"Where your eyes go, you go. Don't look at your feet or off to the side. Keep your eyes and upper body down the slope. The lower body does the turns, but keep your upper body stable."

"I know, I know, I know." This was all what she'd learned in the ski classes Ollie put her in. She hadn't cared for it much back then either.

Graham then leaned to the side. "If you fall to the side, make sure you land with your arm flat. If you land on your elbow, like you are trying to stop your fall, you will pop your collarbone quick—or your arm, but neither feel good. Got it?"

"Check. Breaking bones doesn't feel good."

"If you fall and head toward a tree or a cliff, turn your body and dig your elbows or arms into the snow to slow yourself. Do whatever you can to stop from sliding into a tree."

"Or off a cliff. Check."

Graham looked past the cabin to the slow trail, as if contemplating whether risking an avalanche was better than sending her into the bowl or not. He must have decided he was doing the right thing, because he faced the cliff, adjusting his poles in his hands.

"Follow my trail. I've skied this before and know the best path down."

"Check."

Graham slid over to the starting point. "And, Layla…"

"Yes?"

He turned his eyes toward her, filled with raw emotion that set a fire to Layla's gut. "Make it to the bottom in one piece."

She nodded again, her stomach churning. "Double check."

He looked like he wanted to say more, but he motioned for her to line up behind him.

With one last glance over his shoulder, he tipped off the edge and into the powder, Emmy trailing close behind him.

He made it look easy. Like riding down the street on his bike.

She needed to take off after him before he was too far ahead. And before she threw up. Yet she froze in place, her gasping loud in the unmarked snowy wonderland.

She did the only thing she knew to do. The one thing Ollie would tell her to do. "Oh, God… Help."

A shout sounded from behind the cabin. She was out of time.

She sank forward in her boots and leaned off the edge.

Her stomach dropped, feeling like it was trailing behind as momentum carried her faster. Keeping her body upright, she leaned into her left leg for a parallel turn. Then the right.

She zigzagged, following Graham's tracks. The powder sprayed to the sides, sounding like sand landing on her coat. So far, not so bad.

Then the grade steepened, catapulting her faster. She maintained the zigzag until she couldn't keep up with the speed. Her skis shifted so that they were horizontal to the run, and her balance teetered downhill.

No, no, no. She tipped sideways, gravity heavy. If she fell, she wouldn't be able to stop herself, unless a boulder or a tree stopped her mid-slide. Mustering all her strength, she pressed into her left leg, forcing her skis parallel again.

She could almost hear Graham's instructions echo within her ears: *Keep your body weight forward. Don't let fear force you to lean away.*

She tried to zigzag again but nearly lost control. Halfway down, and trying to slow herself was doing more harm than good. If she wanted to make it down in one piece, she had to lean into the wind and control her direction, if not her speed.

Against every nerve in her body telling her to pull back, she lowered into her boots and gripped her poles harder.

Wind nipped at the bare flesh of her cheeks and yanked at her hood. Panic welled within her gut, but if she gave in, she would crash. So, with a growl low in her throat, she forced herself forward, momentum carrying her faster and faster.

Somehow, she remained on her skis. Maybe she could do this.

Never had she looked her fear in the face and won. It was almost euphoric. Was this rush why adrenaline junkies always found challenges to bring them to the edge?

It made her consider what other fears she could face. And win.

But then a ledge appeared in front of her, with no time to shift course. Her body strained to pull back, but, as if Graham had shouted for her to go for it—and he may have, she couldn't tell—she centered herself on her skis and flew over the ledge.

She felt her stomach drop as she flew midair, unsure of how far off the ground she was. She leaned forward as she braced for the impact of the quickly approaching ground.

She landed with both feet, but the jolt of impact twisted her center of gravity, and the powder seized control of her skis, wrenching them sideways.

With her arms waving to regain control, her body fell to the ground, spraying powder in a wide diameter. Her skis popped off, landing who knew where. She reached out to keep herself from sliding farther, praying a tree or a rock wouldn't be what stopped her.

The fabric of her coat scraped against the snow, the sound of its friction filling the air, until her body finally came to a stop.

FIVE

Graham's mind transported to Anaconda Gulch, as if watching Ollie slide to the edge, helpless. He hadn't been there, but the scene replayed consistently in his nightmares.

He blinked hard. No, not Anaconda. Deadman's Bowl. And not Ollie, but the woman he'd promised to protect.

He couldn't move. He couldn't think. All he could do was watch. The grinding noise of her body sliding across the snow drowned out all other sounds.

She came to a fast halt before slamming into a tree trunk. Layla lay motionless, face down. Her skis skidded into a snow mound twenty feet away. Graham's lungs refused to take in a breath.

Emmy raced to Layla and pawed her arm before nuzzling her nose into her side.

They had been so close to the bottom of the bowl without incident. Even now, her body had landed where the slope leveled out.

Her head lifted.

Air returned to his lungs in a gush, lifting his paralysis. He launched toward her.

"Layla!" he called as he landed on his knees beside her, throwing off his gloves. "Are you okay? Where does it hurt?"

He probed her arms as gentle as his trembling hands would allow, expecting to feel the gruesome cushion of a broken bone. "Where does it hurt, Layla? Can you speak?"

What a fool he'd been to force her down Deadman's Bowl. Maybe traveling under the cornice of snow would have been safer. Had he made the decision based on facts or his own nightmares of being buried alive?

He'd taken her life into his hands. Hands that would have blood on them if she hadn't survived.

She made a funny sound. Almost like a sob but not quite. "I'm fine," she said as she rose to her hands and knees.

"You don't sound fine."

She tilted her head toward him, only then revealing the smile on her face. "I promise, I'm fine."

"Are you laughing?" Graham's body felt stuck between slumping with relief and launching down the mountain without her.

A giggle escaped. "That was awesome."

"Awesome?" Graham sat back on his haunches. "Are you kidding me?"

Layla shook her head as she began to sit up. "Ouch." She stopped moving and brought her hand to her rib cage. "Okay, maybe a little sore."

Graham's mouth tightened as he gripped her elbow to help her to her feet.

Once she stood fully, Graham released her elbow like it had burned him. He grabbed the poles he'd dropped into the powder. "I'll go find your skis."

He stalked away.

Layla lifted her goggles to reveal narrowed eyes. "Hey, I think I did pretty good."

Graham rammed his poles deep into the snow. They wobbled as he let go to point at her. "'Pretty good' will get you killed."

Emmy snorted in agreement. It was good to have Emmy on his side.

He turned to gather her skis once again, but she rushed to block his path. "We made it down. Why are you so miffed?"

Graham squinted and shook his head. She wouldn't understand. Couldn't feel the quaking of his soul.

He drew a long inhale through his nostrils. "You practically gave me a heart attack and then thought it was funny."

She cocked her head. "You were worried about me."

"Well, yeah. I was scared that I failed you by taking this route. I was scared that I'd lost another person that I cared about." The words shoved out of his mouth before they filtered through his brain.

She looked down, a pink hue on her cheeks. From exertion or something else?

A low groan escaped his throat as he picked up her skis. He really needed to control his big mouth.

"Look, Layla…"

Emmy began to bark, her attention somewhere farther down the mountain.

Layla held up a hand. "Shh. Listen."

He stilled, listening to the quiet breeze whistling through the pines. Then he heard it. "A motor."

The hand she held up began to shake. "A snowmobile."

Its motor grew louder. Graham scanned the trees. They were too far off trail for recreational vehicles. Especially after an intense storm.

"He's looking for us." Her voice shuddered. She sounded too certain for him to ignore.

Then, as if solidifying her statement, another motor roared from the other direction. If they didn't move now, they'd be surrounded.

He reached back into his waist band for the gun he stashed. Gone.

His eyes slide closed. He must've lost it coming down the bowl.

Without protection, it was too big of a risk to wait to see who approached. They needed to get out of here.

Graham handed over the ski he held in his hand. "We'll have to make a run for it."

Her body quaked as she tried to put on the skis, her boot slipping past the binding at each attempt. "Run for it? We can't outrun a snowmobile. Especially not when he can follow our tracks."

Tracks that would work as arrows pointing to their every twist and turn. "We don't have a choice."

One of the motors roared louder.

Graham supported her elbow, hoping to stabilize her enough to fit her foot into the binding. "We gotta go, Layla."

His chest tightened. Even the click of Layla's boot fitting into her binding didn't ease the constriction. He held out her other ski. She grabbed it, her pulsating breaths nearing a panic attack.

He slid over to his poles and yanked them out of the snow.

Finally, he heard the click of her other boot as it snapped into its binding. She slid beside him.

He set Emmy on his shoulders and started in the opposite direction of the motor. "Let's go. Stay close."

He made a kick turn to the south, testing to see if the snowmobile would continue to follow. A tourist would stay on their route.

But the motor rumble followed their trail deeper into the woods.

Graham's pulse throbbed beneath his collar, pushing his skis faster.

"Graham!" she shouted as she struggled to keep up with him.

He paused to scan the area. Layla was right: they'd never be able to outrun a snowmobile.

He needed a new plan.

Just ahead, he saw a steep, sudden slope. Before it, a large tree shaded a tall boulder nearby.

It was a crazy idea, but only something crazy would give him the leverage needed.

"Stay directly behind me," he shouted to Layla.

He skied beneath a branch of the tree and lifted Emmy until she climbed atop the boulder.

"Stay!" he shouted before he unclipped his boots from his skis. Reaching up, he grabbed the branch and kicked away his skis down the hill before he swung himself up onto the boulder.

Emmy shifted uneasily. The dog rode ski lifts all day long, the ground looming below, but the boulder made her nervous? "Whoa, girl. It'll be okay."

The pine needles pricked his cheek as he reached his hand down for Layla.

With her eyes fixed on his hand, doubt shadowed her face. "This isn't going to work. He's going to see the skis separate as they go downhill. He's going to know we aren't on them."

"Layla…" Graham's eyes searched hers. "Trust me."

Her mouth tightened, but she didn't argue another word. She gripped his hand and released her bindings with the point of her poles before thrusting her skis down the hill.

After she climbed up beside him, she wrapped her arms securely around Emmy.

The sound of the snowmobile's motor grew closer.

"Now what?" Layla mumbled.

Graham held a finger in front of his lips as he crouched low.

A man dressed in a black coat and red ski mask rode the snowmobile beneath the tree. It stopped directly below them.

Graham held his breath as the stranger raised out of his seat to look down the slope. As he did, the pursuer's coattail lifted up enough to reveal the unmistakable leather of a gun holster.

Graham's pulse hitched. Of course the man would be packing. Which meant he needed to act quickly before the man could pull the gun on them.

The man must've observed how the skis separated down the hill, because he straightened, scoping out the terrain.

Energy coiled in Graham's legs, his hands clasping and unclasping.

Then the man looked up.

Layla saw her reflection in the pursuer's goggles. Cornered.

She closed her eyes, expecting to hear a shot from the gun she'd seen holstered on his belt. But before the blast of a gunshot, Graham sprang off the boulder, landing on top of the man. The snow insulated the sounds of their fall, except for the man's surprised grunt.

The man tried to shout something, but Graham's fist collided with his jaw. With a quick twist of his body, the man crawled out from beneath Graham's grasp. Graham launched himself onto the pursuer's back, hooking his arm around the man's neck, the other around his torso.

The man's arms flailed, trying to find a target, but Graham only tightened his grip.

Layla desperately clung to Emmy who barked

as if torn between protecting Layla and helping Graham.

The longer she sat on the rock, the more she became a sitting target. She had to get out of here.

She slid off the back of the boulder, Emmy following behind. After a brief look toward Graham, who now had the man in a headlock, she straddled the attacker's snowmobile.

"Emmy, come," she called.

Emmy glanced toward Graham, then back at Layla, indecision stuttering her step.

"Emmy, please come."

Emmy shook and started to bark. It made Layla feel like she was being scolded.

What was she thinking, anyway? Graham needed her now. How could she even think of running? Besides, the man would only follow her if she took off. Wouldn't he?

She twisted to look over her shoulder. Somehow the man had gained an advantage, now on top of Graham, with his arm pinned to his back and goggles removed.

Graham lifted his head out of the snow. "Go, Layla. Get out of here!"

"If you would just listen to me!" the man shouted.

The growl in his voice raised the hair on Layla's arm. She couldn't let him get Graham. She couldn't.

She searched her surroundings. What could she do?

Just above her, a dead tree branch extended from

a pine tree. It might work as a weapon if she could get it to snap off.

She stood on the snowmobile's seat and jumped, wrapping her arms around the branch.

With her feet dangling off the ground, she jounced her body until the limb cracked. Only one more and the branch broke, tossing her into the powder.

Before she could change her mind, she loaded the branch over her shoulder like a bat and swung it into the man's back.

He teetered, but the force only loosened his grip. Even so, it was enough for Graham to shift out of the hold and roll away, then gain the upper hand.

In one swift motion, Graham ripped off the man's ski mask and goggles.

His arms went limp, staring into a red-faced man who glared back at Graham.

It wasn't Flint; that much, Layla knew.

Graham narrowed his eyes and yanked on the man's jacket. "Zane. I knew it."

"I tried to tell you it was me, but you wouldn't stop."

"I wouldn't have stopped if I had known it was you."

The men glared at each other, all the while their huffs filling the silence.

"Let me up, Graham."

"No, not until you tell me why you were chasing us."

Zane rolled his eyes. "Why? How about the fact

that you never clocked out yesterday? Your car was still in the lot. I figured you were caught in the storm. I'm a first responder, Graham. I was looking for you. Although now I wonder why I even bothered."

Layla inched forward, Emmy sticking close by. "You aren't after me?"

"Ma'am, I don't even know who you are. Why would I be after you?"

"You don't work for Cameron?"

Zane's jaw twitched. As if the name triggered a reaction. A hint that he knew something? Still, as he stood, his eyes took on a nonchalant glaze. He shoved Graham away. "Cameron who?"

Maybe being on the run was playing with Layla's imagination. The man couldn't possibly know anything.

"Why are you carrying a gun?" Graham asked.

Zane huffed. "I have a permit."

After examining Zane, Graham jerked his head toward him. "Tell him, Layla."

Her tongue stuck to the roof of her mouth. Why would she trust this man? Especially when Graham obviously didn't?

Graham folded his arms, his gaze not turning from Zane. "May as well tell him, Layla. He already knows something's up."

Her face flushed; she wished she could hide. She refused to divulge her whole story, which Zane would probably demand. He looked like a "don't beat around the bush" type guy. Not so different from Graham. Maybe that's why they didn't get along. But maybe she could keep from telling him the key pieces.

She took a sharp inhale. "Cameron Flint."

Zane raised his eyebrows. "You mean, the district attorney?"

There it was again—the nagging feeling that he wasn't surprised at all. "Yeah."

Zane shifted and folded his arms. "Why would you be afraid of him?"

She glanced over at Graham, but he took on the same posture as Zane.

She could lie. Too bad she couldn't get Ollie's disappointed face out of her mind. "We had a disagreement, and I'm trying to avoid him." Totally true.

Zane widened his stance. "So you ran from me, shoved your skis downhill and jumped on me—not to mention almost stole my snowmobile—because you want to avoid Flint? I'm not buying it."

Layla's face heated. "I *really* want to avoid him."

Zane poked his finger toward his snowmobile. "Or you wanted to steal my snowmobile."

"Hey!" Graham clenched his fists at his side. "Who do you think I am? You know me better than that."

"Do I, Graham? Ever since Ollie died, you've been a hothead. I don't trust you."

"The feeling is mutual," Graham said through gritted teeth.

Both men glared at each other, fists at the ready.

If she didn't do something, the fight from earlier would resume.

"Because Flint wants me dead."

There. She'd said it, but the way Zane tilted his head, calculating and cold, made her regret it. Disbelief. The one reaction she could read as well as words on a page.

"Why would he want you dead? Who are you, again?"

"You don't need her name. Just know that Flint isn't the man you think he is."

Zane acted like he hadn't heard Graham. "What is your name?"

"Like I said, you don't need to know. Now that you know I'm alive, Dudley Do-Right, you can move on with your day."

That is when she heard it: the other motor. And it was close.

"Your name." A new edge sharpened Zane's voice.

"Why do you need to know?" Graham stepped toward him.

The motor roared closer.

"Why won't you tell me?"

"She doesn't have to tell you if she doesn't want to."

The snowmobile was nearly there. Its rumble sounded just over the ridge.

"Layla. Layla Quin," she shouted.

Zane's mouth tightened. "Ollie's sister." With a quick glimpse toward the ridge, he jerked his head toward his own snowmobile. "Quick. You gotta get her outta here. Take the snowmobile. Leave the skis."

"Why were you looking for me two years ago out by the bridge just outside the event center?" Layla couldn't help but blurt out despite the urgency.

Zane looked stunned. "I don't know what you are talking about."

"It was the night before the fall festival. I was hiding under the bridge and your truck stopped on it, looking for me. Why were you looking for me?"

Zane's jaw went slack. "If we are talking of the same night, it wasn't you I was looking for. Now go!"

Layla ran toward the snowmobile, Emmy on her tail. When Graham didn't follow, she looked over her shoulder. He hadn't moved, hands clenched in fists at his sides.

"Why?" he asked.

"Graham, for once in your life, take orders. Get her out of here!"

"Let's go, Graham."

Graham's gaze bounced between Zane and her, indecision stiffening his movements.

Finally, he jabbed a finger toward Zane. "We are not through here. You have some explaining to do."

Zane's face was cryptic. "Agreed. Now, git!"

Graham straddled the seat in front of Layla as she held on tightly to Emmy in the middle.

"And, Graham," Zane called, "trust no one. Anyone could be working with Flint."

Graham hesitated. Layla saw his throat bob as he swallowed before he revved up the motor.

The snowmobile lunged forward. With her arms around Emmy, Layla gripped Graham's coat to keep the momentum from tossing them backward.

Graham sped down the same slope they had just tossed their skis down. Gravity dragged them faster, causing Layla's stomach to lurch.

She glanced over her shoulder just as another snowmobile launched off the top of the hill with what seemed like a limitless hang time. The skilled driver landed effortlessly, his pursuit unhindered.

Layla nudged Graham. "Faster!"

Graham leaned forward over the handlebars, pushing the throttle harder.

Layla's pulse pounded in her ears, almost out-drumming the combination of the motors. She hunched over Emmy, willing the snowmobile to pick up speed.

A pop filled the air. Layla recoiled, hearing the bullet whiz past her ear.

Leaning to the side, she reached her arm around Graham and pressed his hand into the throttle, only to find that he already had the pedal to the metal.

Another shot shattered the air. She lost her balance, her body drifting off the side of the vehicle. Letting go of the throttle, Graham swung his arm behind him to catch her. The mobile decelerated as the other vehicle got closer.

Using his arm, she balanced herself back on her

seat and folded her body over Emmy's as Graham hit the throttle once more.

"Hang on!" Graham called. "We are almost to the marked slopes. Hopefully, he'll back off with spectators around."

Desperate for something to help him go faster, she pressed into him, squishing Emmy.

More shots were fired behind them. Her body flinched with each one but didn't register any pain.

"Uh-oh," he muttered.

"Uh-oh? Worse than gunfire?"

Before he could answer, the mobile launched off a berm, twisting in the air. Graham's hands struggled to maintain their grip on the steering wheel as it wobbled.

Layla braced for impact, trying to hold Emmy in place. The snowmobile struck the ground, slamming Layla's teeth together. Momentum spun the mobile into orange boundary tape, wrapping it around them.

Finally, the vehicle slowed, balancing on its right blade before pounding back down into the packed snow.

Then all was silent.

SIX

The spray of snow showered slush into the top of Graham's boot as the snowmobile skidded to a stop, soaking his already crusty socks.

He didn't move, his hands clenching the rubber grips of the handlebars.

The hissing motor puttered, then died, but somehow his arms were still vibrating.

The roar of the other snowmobile revved off in the opposite direction. Probably chased away by the mix of skiers circling around them.

At least, for now. Graham's gut said he'd be back.

If only he'd caught a glimpse of the man's face. It couldn't be the man they'd left tied up on the mountain. A man with a head wound couldn't ride or shoot like that. Unless he was superhuman.

No, it must've been someone else. So how many guys did Flint have working for him?

Zane's warning echoed in his head: *Trust no one. Anyone could be working with Flint.*

Graham was fighting an enemy he couldn't see. Couldn't recognize.

Meaning, he might just fail.

Framed in the mobile's cracked windshield, the sign identifying Alpha Peak's green Rambling Slope stood, contrasting with the intensity brewing in his veins. His insides strained with the same tension of a triple black diamond.

Voices of skiers mumbled as they inched closer, as if he had just flown in on a space capsule from another planet. He tried to turn the key. They had to get out of here, but the motor only sputtered.

Flooded? Maybe. Probably. Of course. He tried again.

"Hey, what's the big idea?" a stranger shouted. "You could have killed someone."

"How did he get a red patrol coat? He needs to be reported," another said.

A chorus of agreements surrounded him, except for one man standing with his arms crossed—unrecognizable beneath his goggles and helmet.

Graham turned the key again, his focus not straying from the stranger.

Nothing.

He reached back to touch Layla. He could feel her warmth radiate from behind, so he knew she hadn't flown off. Still, she was motionless. And quiet. Too quiet.

"You okay, Layla?"

The silence trapped the wind in his chest. Until her own deep inhale and nearly inaudible, "Yes," allowed him to breathe again.

"Is Emmy okay?"

Emmy answered with a whine.

"She's fine. I think. Can we just get out of here?"

The engine refused to turn over. A few skiers decided not to waste the day and dispersed, but the ones who remained pointed their phones at him, taking pictures or murmuring disgust.

It was more than claustrophobic panic setting in. It was the realization that any one of these people could be working for Flint, ready to follow them.

Going on foot was not an option.

If only the engine would start.

For the first time since losing Ollie, one option popped into his mind. He closed his eyes, blocking the commotion around him. "God, I could really use Your help to start this engine. Not for me, but for Layla?" Like a whisper from the past, he could almost hear Ollie reminding him to pray.

He blew out a puff of air before he turned the igniter again. The engine choked, but it seemed to pulse a little faster than the last time. "Please, God." He tried one more time.

The engine awakened with a roar. Layla tangibly relaxed behind him. "Let's go!"

He pressed the throttle, directing the mobile down the slope, a tail of boundary tape flapping in the wind behind them.

When they were nearly at the bottom of the slope, close to the Chamberlain lift on the north side of the resort, another snowmobile driven by a man in a red patrol coat cut them off.

"Graham, what do you think you're doing? I had a call that a patroller barged a snowmobile across the boundary. You know snowmobiles are forbidden here. Zane would have your hide."

"Jim…" He didn't point out the irony that he was riding Zane's mobile—a mobile that sputtered and died once again.

"I've got people breathing down my neck to call the police."

Graham took his time dismounting the vehicle, his eyes scoping out the area. Could he trust Jim? He wanted to. After all, Jim had been there for him since high school. He was one of the few Graham had told about his mom leaving, and he'd responded with compassion.

"Look—" Graham stepped toward Jim "—there's been trouble. I've got to get this girl outta here. Can you cover for me?"

Jim's eyes narrowed; he was ready to jump to his defense. "Trouble? What kind of trouble?"

See? Jim was his friend. Still, he would keep information to only the essentials. No sense endangering Jim unless necessary. "I'll fill you in later. I just need you to cover for me. Say I had a family emergency or something."

"Zane is already out looking for you."

Which was weird. He couldn't possibly care. Although, he had "loaned" him the snowmobile to escape with Layla. "Yep. I know."

Two other patrollers approaching from a different slope stole Jim's attention. "You better get out of here, or you'll be detained for questioning."

Graham reached out for Layla. Her small hand gripped his with surprising strength. "Let's go."

She didn't answer as she followed him past the lodge.

He weaved through the crowd of people milling around the lodge. Most of their looks were merely curious, but the attention made him itch.

He started for the parking lot, then stopped. With a shake of his head, he changed course toward the gondola. "We can't take my Jeep. I lost my bumper on Switchback Trail last summer and never thought it was worth the money to replace. It would be recognized driving around town."

Layla grimaced. "We won't stick out any less riding the gondola."

Graham hesitated at the truth. Especially in his bright red patrol coat.

He glanced around and ducked behind a large van, then slid off his coat. "We'll have to try to blend in."

He pulled the sleeves of his coat inside out, revealing the black inner lining. People may wonder why he was wearing his coat inside out, but at least they wouldn't recognize it as a patrol coat. Then he undid Emmy's harness and strapped it on backward to hide her badges.

When he was finished, he grabbed Layla's hand again. "Let's go."

They made their way around the other side of the lodge, Emmy close at their heels. The line for the gondola weaved around the ropes with more sightseers than skiers. Layla looped her arm through his and directed him to the back of the line.

Graham's gaze jumped from one person to another, his body tensed for an attack. One man dug into his pocket. With one arm, Graham shoved Layla behind him, but the man pulled out a cell phone, not a gun.

Conversations milled around him, grating against his resolve to remain calm. No one realized the danger lurking in the trees.

A man behind them grumbled, "I don't remember the last time the deer population was so heavy. Nearly hit one again out there on the highway. Would've dented my Benz."

Graham rolled his eyes. He'd take a deer problem and dented Benz any day over running for his life.

"Yeah," said the other man. "They're everywhere. I nearly hit one a week ago too."

The cords in Graham's neck bunched. Maybe these men worked for Flint and were trying to distract him.

He flinched when Layla touched his arm. "Stop acting so intense," she whispered. "You're only going to draw attention."

Emmy whimpered and pressed against his leg, as if she, too, didn't know who to trust. "Do you realize that any of these people could work for Flint?" Graham said to Layla.

Her smile contrasted with the seriousness in her eyes. "I've wondered that myself the past two years trying to stay alive." She leaned closer. "The only way to blend in is to look like you don't have a care in the world."

Tough chance of that. He had bigger problems than deer crossing the road.

She reached up and cupped his cheek. He forced his eyes not to close at her touch. How did she expect him to stay alert? "What are you doing?"

Her gaze tangled with his. A look that about buckled his knees. "If we act cozier, like maybe we're in love, then it makes people uncomfortable enough to turn away."

"And how do you know this?" He didn't have to act for his voice to sound so husky. Having her this close did that to him.

The line inched forward. "I don't. But it's worth a shot."

A multitude of doubts argued in his head, but already the guys behind him seemed to take a step back.

Well, he *would* do anything to keep her safe.

He draped his arm around her back and pulled her close. She hesitated, then leaned her head into him, as if he could shield her from gunmen and corrupt DAs.

A strong realization rolled over him. No longer was this about protecting Ollie's sister. No, this was about her. Someone he cared deeply about.

Graham startled when the guy behind him spoke. "Hey, do you mind? You're holding up the line."

Layla inhaled sharply as she pulled away. Without glancing toward him, she twined her fingers through his, and he followed her to bridge the gap in the line.

Graham blew out a breath. Wow. Her nearness did have a way of easing the tightness in his chest.

She leaned her back into him as they waited, and he couldn't help but notice how she fit so perfectly. Tilting her head up to look at him, she whispered, "You're a good actor."

Actor. Right. Someone should tell that to his pounding heart, which he was ready to serve to her on a silver platter. She could win an Emmy for her performance. No pun intended.

His heart squeezed. With her warmth flooding his skin, he could almost believe someone might love him enough to stick around. Or at least take a chance on him.

His tongue stuck to the roof of his mouth, but he managed to say, "You too."

They neared the front of the line, the gentle hum of the gondola's engine loud enough to cover any conversation. Once they stepped into the gondola, a family of four sat on the bench opposite them, the air stiff with discomfort.

Layla stared out the window, avoiding his gaze, but that was fine with him. How could he ever look her in the eye again without revealing how her nearness had unbalanced him? How could he pretend the moment had meant nothing?

At least she was right that people seemed to not pay attention. Even the family across from them was focused on each other or out the window, except for the occasional glance toward Emmy, who seemed to ignore the attention.

As the family *ooh*ed and *aah*ed over the treed mountainside and the moose grazing in the snowy meadow below them, he gathered his wits.

He had one job to do: keep Layla safe. If he allowed emotion to distract him, he would fail.

And failure meant Layla would die.

Graham's embrace had flipped something within Layla. Like a light illuminating how alone she'd been the past two years.

She followed Graham across the bridge from the gondola station to the main drag of Silver Ridge. The midday sun had melted the storm's inches into a muddy slush.

They hadn't spoken much, but the feel of his arm around her was still warm on her skin. An embrace that probably hadn't affected him the way it had her.

What would it be like to have someone always be by her side? Someone to stand up for her?

She gave her head a small shake, trying to let go of the longing that would only disappoint her in the end. She'd do best to remember he was only a friend.

Besides, the longer she prolonged leaving— hopefully with Emmy—the more danger she put Graham in. Even if the idea of leaving his side, the one person who understood her, gutted her strength and left her bare. How selfish could she be?

A worker in a green coat with a Silver Ridge patch scooped the sidewalk, the shovel's scrape against concrete an accompaniment to the voices of tourists milling in and out of the shops.

The historic mining town that had been re-created into a world-class ski village boasted an ambience like no other. Some buildings still had the original planked storefronts, now painted in pastel blues and yellows and mixed in with the more modern brick structures trimmed in evergreen and purple.

Emmy—now leashed, as per city code—whimpered as they passed a grill, the aroma of sizzling steak and hamburgers floating out to the sidewalk. Layla's stomach flipped, and she resisted letting out a whimper of her own.

Graham led her by the hand through town. She really should ask where they were going, but his hand was warm, his strength contagious. And much to her dismay, she trusted him.

Until he led her to a large stucco building sitting back two blocks west of Main Street.

The sheriff's station.

Layla's feet planted on the sidewalk. Yep, trusting him had been a mistake.

"What are we doing here?" The squeak in her voice drew attention from a woman in yoga pants and faux-fur boots passing them on the sidewalk.

Layla stepped closer and lowered her voice. "Why did you bring me here?"

"Because my cell phone is dead, and we have

to talk to someone. Living on the run is no way to live, Layla."

The white stucco-and-stone sheriff's station didn't look so scary, with its wooden beams and large windows. It had the aura of a community center, but Layla still shivered. The last time she met with law enforcement, the officers had looked at her like she was a poor rebellious child, disbelieving her story. Nothing would be different this time.

She began to back away. "It's my choice. I won't tell anyone."

Graham reached for her arm before she could escape. When she faced him, she saw the weight of her own burden he had taken on. "I was hoping you changed your mind. Remember all that 'what if' talk back at the cabin?"

"There is no way they will believe me."

"You don't know that."

"Yes I do." How could she make him understand? She hated the tears burning her eyes. "I'm a nobody, Graham. I fade into a crowd, no one pays attention to me. It's where I belong. Cameron Flint is high profile, the type everyone knows and trusts. If I accuse him, not only will they laugh at me, but I suddenly become a person of interest, and I can't blend in anymore. To stay alive, I have to blend in."

Graham entwined his fingers through hers. "Well, I see you, and I think you deserve to live the life you want, not blending in because you are afraid. You are a whole lot stronger than you think, Layla."

Would he ever understand how helpless she was against someone so powerful? "I can't stop him, Graham. Please let me disappear. If you let me have Emmy, at least I won't be alone anymore."

Graham gazed toward the mountain beyond, the scars of the slopes dripping down through the trees. "We can't see Deadman's Bowl from here. You were afraid then too."

"Graham, it's not the same thing."

"You went down because it was the only way. Maybe this is the only way. And maybe the freedom will allow you to laugh again, just like you laughed at the bottom of Deadman's Bowl."

"Or I will be dead."

Graham shrugged. "You could've been dead at the bottom of Deadman's Bowl too. Point is, you are stronger than you think you are. Why won't you fight? You deserve to be free."

Graham's image blurred as tears crowded her vision. She wanted to believe him, but he hadn't seen the frustration in the cops' eyes as they accused her of shoplifting. They hadn't believed her then; they wouldn't believe her now. Not when her story included the prestigious Cameron Flint.

She took a step back, pulling her hand out of his grip. "I'm sorry, I can't."

His expression pleaded for her not to run. "Give this a chance. How about I went in there and found Deputy Dillinger? He's a good guy. Went to church with Ollie and me. In fact, they were buds. I can have him meet you somewhere and then see what he thinks you should do. Unofficial, remember?"

She started to shake her head to say no, but the hope reflected on his face stopped her.

She inhaled a long, slow breath. What if they met in a place she could easily escape from? Say, somewhere outside city limits? And if the officer came on foot, not on or in anything that made him faster than her, then maybe she could appease Graham. "He'll probably say I need to file a report."

"Again, you don't know that."

The sounds of the street rushed around them as Graham waited for an answer. It was pointless, but it might be the only way for Graham to see there was no other way.

"Okay, but we have to meet over by the river." That way she could find the bridge with the ledge she'd once hidden under, in case she needed to escape.

Graham smiled. "Deal." He reached out to shake her hand.

She hesitated, then accepted his hand. Wow, the man did funny things to her heart.

A sensation of free falling rolled over her, not unlike tipping over the edge into Deadman's Bowl again, adrenaline fused and out of control.

Which only meant the quicker she made her escape from him, the better. For if there was one thing she couldn't do, it was lose control. Become reckless. Recklessness, no matter how innocent, could get him killed.

Besides, she didn't deserve happy endings. It was only a matter of time before he decided she was bad news and not worth the risk.

Graham motioned to the building. "I'll meet you back there in the alley behind the station and let you know what he says."

She shouldn't. Really. But she heard herself say, "Okay."

Clearing her throat, she moved toward the alley, but he pulled her back close.

"Layla…" Intensity weighted his voice, matching the tightness of his mouth.

"Yes?"

"Don't leave without saying goodbye."

His eyes said so much more than his words, but she couldn't decipher it. Did he simply want to know when she'd leave? Or was there more to his request that she didn't understand?

Again, she wondered what had happened with his mom.

She held his gaze. She shouldn't promise. Not when she lived moment by moment. Even so, she said, "I promise."

He hesitated, his eyes dropping to her mouth, but, just as quickly, he let go of her hand and started for the building's door.

Layla watched until his broad-shouldered frame disappeared through the glass door. Emmy nudged her leg. With a sharp inhale, Layla scanned the area and skirted around to the alley before anyone noticed her loitering on the sidewalk.

She wanted to run into the alley, to sprint into the protection it would provide. But she reined herself to a walk to keep from drawing attention.

She rounded the corner and leaned against the stucco wall, as invisible as she could make herself.

Emmy looked at her with amber eyes, as if monitoring her well-being.

Oh, she'd missed her dog. She smiled down at her and ran a hand over her ears.

The crunch of hardened snow and mud echoed through the alley. Layla's hand froze in Emmy's fur.

A car.

She pressed her back into the building and waited for it to pass, but the car stopped, blocking the most logical exit.

Layla's pulse thrummed in her ears. Did they see her? Would they even care if they did?

It could be a county official or someone delivering something to the station, but wariness clawed at her stomach.

A tall man, his face covered by a ski mask stepped out of the driver's seat. He turned, slow, methodical, until his gaze collided with hers.

Unable to breathe, she dragged her body along the jagged stucco, away from the man, hoping the shadows eclipsed her escape.

Until the stranger raised a gun and aimed it at her.

The sun reflected off the metal as Layla gasped. Slowly, she raised her arms and backed up a step.

If only she could reach her Mace. Somehow hide

it in her hand until the stranger approached. But she couldn't draw it out faster than a bullet.

She took another step back. Then another. The gunman didn't come near. He simply stared at her, murder in his eyes.

If she continued to back up, maybe she could use the dumpster as a shield. Maybe escape around the corner of the building.

She took another step back, but behind her, more wheels ground through the ice, rolling to a stop. The hairs on the nape of her neck raised.

In her periphery, she saw that a gray clunker had pulled across the alleyway's other exit.

Her eyesight blurred as the other driver, also in a mask, stepped out and pointed a gun at her.

Her sight bounced from man to man, her heart rate erratic.

Trapped. Nowhere to run.

The Mace in her pocket hung heavy, but she'd be gunned down before she could even pull it out.

Beside her, Emmy crouched low, a throaty growl rumbling.

The men approached from either side, precise and in sync. It created a vacuum of air, and Layla's head spun.

Emmy's growl intensified.

One of the men aimed his gun at Emmy. "Tie the dog up."

Layla squeezed the leash.

"Now! Or your pooch will play catch with my bullet."

Every muscle in Layla quaked. Made it almost impossible to tie the leash around a pipe attached to the building.

"Good. Now, don't move." The man signaled to the other. "My partner here is going to zip-tie your hands, and you'll let him. Unless you want me to kill your dog."

Emmy started to bark, straining against her tether. Layla didn't even flinch as the other man wrenched the zip tie around her wrists in front of her torso.

"That's real good." The man jerked his head toward his car. "Now, get in the trunk."

SEVEN

Graham was in trouble. Wasn't falling for his dead friend's sister against some kind of code?

Not to mention it upped the stakes. After all, no longer was he simply fighting to free Ollie's sister from a powerful man. Now he was fighting for the one woman he might be willing to take a chance on.

His chest constricted as he walked into the sheriff's station. The hustle of the deputies and civilians stirred the lobby with urgency. The pulse in his neck quickened.

He needed one of the good guys on Layla's side. Just one to convince her to testify. It was wrong for a man to get away with murder simply because of his position.

He strode up to the administration desk, very aware that he didn't smell much better than the ski bum cuffed to the bench. "I'm here to see Deputy Matt Dillinger. Is he available?"

A female deputy with short, curly hair looked at him with suspicious eyes. "He is busy, sir. Anything I can help you with?"

"I need his advice. I'm sort of a friend."

"You will have to call and make an appointment."

"I don't have his number."

"Then maybe you aren't the 'sort of' friends you thought you were."

Graham leaned into the desk and lowered his voice. "Look, I just waited out the storm in a back-country ski shack because a madman was shooting at me. I need to talk with him."

The deputy's brow pinched. Now she was understanding. But, with a sympathetic look, she said, "If you'll wait, we can get you started on making a report."

Graham took a breath. "I'd rather ask Deputy Dillinger if he can squeeze me in for five—"

"Graham McAllister?"

Graham turned to see the deputy walking through the lobby with a file in his hand. Graham's lungs deflated. "Deputy Dillinger, I need to speak with you."

The deputy's eyes flitted between Graham and the deputy behind the admin desk, as if he was about to tell him the same thing: *Fill out a report.*

Graham squeezed the bridge of his nose. "Please, Matt. I need only a few minutes. A friend is in danger."

Deputy Dillinger tipped up his chin, his scrutiny tangible. "What's going on? It's not like you to be so insistent."

Graham inhaled to keep his voice calm. "We have been outrunning a shooter since yesterday, right before the storm hit. That has a tendency to put me under some stress."

Something passed over the deputy's face; he finally had his attention. "Who's 'we'?"

Layla's name stuck to the roof of his mouth. She would take off running for sure if he said her name for the entire county sheriff's department to hear. He leaned closer to Matt and whispered, "Can we talk somewhere in private? Not for me, but for Ollie."

Deputy Dillinger's eyes flitted over to the deputy behind the desk with some sort of silent communication before he looked back at Graham. "What does Ollie have to do with this?"

Graham tightened his mouth.

The deputy heaved a sigh. "Fine, follow me."

Graham followed Dillinger down a hall and into a conference room.

The deputy sat across from Graham and folded his hands on the table, his posture stiff. "Now, tell me, what is going on?"

Graham scratched his bearded jaw. "Yesterday, near the end of my shift, I followed someone suspicious past the boundary, which turned out to be someone I knew. A friend, actually. I barely had a chance to ask questions when someone started shooting at us."

Dillinger clicked his pen. "Do you have a description of the shooter?"

"No, he stayed hidden in the trees. We fled on skis, deeper into the backcountry. Turns out, my friend had witnessed a murder two years ago here in Silver Ridge and has been on the run since."

Matt's eyebrows shot up. Finally, the alarmed response Graham had been hoping for.

Matt scribbled something down on a notepad. "Who was the victim?"

Graham rubbed his hands along his pants. This would be so much more effective if he had a name. "She's not sure."

Yep, Matt's shoulders sagged. "I need the victim's name. Otherwise, she may not have seen what she thought she did."

"Can't you look up missing persons from within that time frame or something?"

"I could if this is an actual lead."

Graham could see it then, the skepticism in the lines of Dillinger's brow. Skepticism that probably accompanied being a deputy. After all, he saw more than Graham could imagine. But that didn't mean he should put Layla in the position of being scrutinized and tagged as a troublemaker.

Matt tapped his pen on the paper. "What happened after you skied deeper into the backcountry? Did the perpetrator follow you?"

Graham studied the black ballpoint pen in Dillinger's hand. He shifted. "Um, yeah, he did. We ran into the storm to get away from him."

Matt wrote something, the scribbles illegible from where Graham sat. "Where did you run to? Did the perpetrator follow you there?"

"We took cover in Lone Man's Hut. Then the next morning—"

Matt's cell began to ring. He looked at it and set down his pen. "Excuse me for a minute."

He stood and stepped out of the conference room. Graham smoothed his palms along the arm of the chair and blew out a breath. Matt's muffled voice filtered from the hallway.

A bad feeling seeped into Graham's gut. Something wasn't right. Maybe it was the hushed tone Matt used, or maybe it was the way he glanced through the door at Graham before he took a couple more steps away.

The urge to hear what Matt was saying pulsed through his veins. He really shouldn't eavesdrop— especially on a sheriff's deputy—but it wouldn't hurt to know the nature of the call.

Graham raised out of his seat and moved against the wall to where he could hear but not be seen.

"—where did you say? The district attorney's office?"

Ice slithered down Graham's limbs.

"What was stolen?"

Dillinger responded with predictable *mmm-hmm*s and *okay*s. The call was nearing its end, so Graham started to go back to his seat—until he heard, "And the DA has proof that it was this Layla Quin."

Graham froze as his mind raced through everything he had just said to Dillinger. At no point had he given the deputy her name. He was almost certain.

"Sounds like tight evidence. We need to bring her in for questioning. And where did he say she was last seen?"

The accusation punched Graham in the gut. He'd made a terrible mistake. Now Flint didn't have just his minions watching for Layla but also law enforcement. The good guys. If they knew she was hiding in the alley behind the building, would they arrest her?

And he'd led her right to them.

Why hadn't he listened to her? Cameron Flint had the law under his control.

He didn't have time to beat himself up. He had to get Layla out of there. To where, he didn't know.

By the time Dillinger came back into the room, Graham was seated, but he couldn't have looked natural. Not with the sweat building on his forehead and stiff smile.

Dillinger narrowed his eyes as he clipped his cell back to his belt. "Sorry about that. You okay?"

"Yeah, sure. I've just been thinking, the shooter is long gone, and we made it unscathed. He probably won't be back."

The deputy crossed his arms. "Really?"

"Yeah, you know, probably just a prank of some kind." He stood. "I've wasted enough of your time."

Dillinger didn't move away from the door to let Graham out. "That is a quick change of heart. What's going on?"

Graham shrugged. "I simply had time to think about the whole thing, and I can see why it sounds hard to believe. But wacky pranks happen on the slopes."

Dillinger's gaze narrowed, his thoughts covertly hidden from his face. A technique he'd probably perfected in training.

With a sigh, he moved to his side of the table and picked up the notepad he had written on. After a quick glance, he hovered the pen over the paper. "What was the witness's name, again?"

Graham backed up toward the door. "Not sure if it matters. Just an acquaintance."

Then he exited like a guilty man who needed to get away. But he didn't care. He had to get Layla out of there.

Now it was up to him to prove Flint's guilt.

His pulse pounded for him to move faster through the sheriff's station, but he forced himself to stay at a steady clip. He even waved at the deputy at the front desk.

Near the front door, a dog barked incessantly in the distance. Just a dog, or Emmy?

His chest squeezed. Oh, no.

He burst free of the front door and ran to the back alley. He didn't even care if someone followed him.

"Layla?"

His gaze swept over the alley. It was empty. Except for Emmy, who flailed against her leash, which was tied to a pipe. Layla would never tie Emmy up. Unless coerced to do so.

His gut lurched as he hurried over to her. "Emmy. I'm here, girl. What happened?"

Once free, she encircled his feet, whimpering. Something terrible had happened.

"Layla!"

He hunched over, bracing his hands on his knees. She was gone.

If Layla couldn't get her pulse under control, she may as well give up. And giving up was not an option. Not when she'd survived this long.

She inhaled through her nose. Okay, she needed to list the things she knew. See if anything would give her an edge.

There was only one man. She'd heard the other gunman through the trunk say he would meet her driver at the rendezvous point. Which meant if she waited to escape, she'd be fighting at least two men instead of one. Maybe three, if Flint was there.

The vehicle made a sharp turn to the right. The momentum slammed her body against a pile of junk lining the trunk. She couldn't see it in the murky darkness, but it stank like garbage. At least it softened the impact.

The car straightened back out.

Back to her list. She might not know the rendezvous place, but she felt the car turn left out of the parking lot and believed it still headed south. That didn't help. It meant she only had a few miles between town and the mountain pass. Meaning, if she was going to escape, she needed to do it soon, before the roadway became bordered by sheer cliffs.

The stickiness of blood trickled down her wrists. She'd squirmed enough for her restraints to slice into her skin. Bruises lined her legs from where she'd banged and kicked against the trunk to no avail.

She'd failed to kick out the taillight or anything that might unlatch the trunk. Nor had her thumping alerted any passersby. Nothing worked.

Her gut squeezed tight. She might not make it out of this one alive.

She hated the tear sliding down her cheek. She shoved again with her legs, even though they trembled with weakness. What else could she do?

The rancid smell crawled over skin. There was nothing. Not even the Mace in her coat pocket could save her.

Shivers quaked her body. She'd never given up. Not before. But now…

Like a siren from her past, Ollie's voice flooded her ears. A memory of when she'd quaked on the side of a mountain, unable to make the last ski run. She'd been so tired. Spent.

Ollie had lowered his goggles and said to her, *Layla, don't give up now. When you don't feel like you have the strength, pray. Allow God to be your strength when you have nothing left.*

More tears rippled before her eyes.

Oh, Ollie. She missed him so much.

She'd prayed on the run, but God had seemed so distant. Like He was watching but was indifferent to her cries.

Or was it she who had kept God at arm's length? Praying, but not really expecting Him to hear?

It didn't matter now. All she knew was, in this moment, only God could get her out of this.

She squeezed her eyes shut. *Father, I need help.*

They were the only words she could force past her trembling lips. Nothing dramatic or flashy happened, but a peace covered her like a blanket. She grasped hold of that peace and let it soothe her quaking insides.

At least until the car lurched to the right, flinging Layla's body toward the back of the trunk. Squealing brakes shrilled loudly through the air as the car swerved.

Layla scrambled to brace her legs against the walls of the trunk, but she couldn't secure herself before the car careened into something hard. Immovable. Her body launched into the mound of trash.

She groaned as she rolled onto her back. What happened?

She heard her captor release a string of choice words from the driver's seat. She couldn't hear them all, but he said something about how he should've just hit the deer and not the snow berm.

Layla gasped. *A deer.*

Exhaust hissed from the front of the car. The engine choked as her captor tried to start the car.

The man shouted a curse word. He tried again, but it still wouldn't start.

A new fight began to tingle in her limbs.

The driver's-side door opened as he grumbled some more. If he was coming for her, she didn't have long.

With her hands still tied together, she twisted until she could fumble her fingers into her pocket to grasp the Mace.

The metal tube was cold as she clutched it, and she began to wrench it out from her coat's fabric. It started to slip.

Boots clumped along the pavement toward the trunk. Her breath came in gasps. She clenched her fingers tighter around the Mace. If she dropped it, she'd never be able to find it before her captor opened the trunk.

It started to slip even more. She contorted her wrists, grinding her jaw against the pain of her restraints carving into her sores, and caught it.

Keys rattled just outside the trunk, and she situated the cylinder in her hand.

She'd just positioned her finger when the trunk lid sprang open.

Without waiting for her captor to reach for her, she squeezed the nozzle, spraying the Mace directly at him.

His shriek pierced her ears as he clutched his face with his hands.

With weak knees, she stumbled out of the trunk. As she did, he reached out an arm to grab her, but he misjudged the distance, and she maneuvered around him.

With hands still bound in front, she took off down the side of the road, her captor yelling. She ignored his cries and forced her legs faster.

A gunshot rang out. Layla flinched, but the bullet clipped the side of the tree. She pressed on faster.

Another shot, but it, too, fired wide. She thought she heard him running behind her, but when she turned her head, she didn't see him.

A country road branched off to the left. She took the turn and kept running.

She crossed a bridge over a stream. Oh, she wanted to drink the cold water for her parched throat, but she didn't dare.

She might, however, follow the stream and evade her pursuer with the unexpected move.

Making her choice in a split second, she ran along the banks of the stream, then jumped across to try to hide her footprints.

She landed, but her right leg splashed into the stream. The chill of the water pierced her skin like needles.

No longer able to press through the exhaustion of her body, she slowed, her steps stumbling to a halt. Now what?

Shivers ransacked her body. Somehow, she had to find someplace warm before hypothermia set in. And soon. The way her damp foot ached, she could be heading toward frostbite.

She had only one person she could trust: Graham.

Didn't he say he still lived in the same condo not too far down from Beta Peak? She'd been there enough times with Ollie that she could find it.

Probably.

Desperate for his warmth, to feel his arms around her, she forced her feet forward. She followed the river to the nearest bridge, where she crested the embankment, then followed another county road back toward town.

Her toes dragged in the plowed dirt; she was unable to lift them anymore.

On autopilot, she made it to Graham's street as dusk darkened the horizon. Through the dim light, she could see his condo building ahead at the top of the hill. Almost there.

A wail of sirens split the air as a police car careened down the street. Screeching to a halt, it parked in front of Graham's building.

Then another just like it did the same.

Panic seized her heart. What was going on? Was Graham okay?

New energy surged through her muscles as her pulse stammered. Images of Graham being hurt flooded her mind.

Oh, no. What had she done?

She had to get to him. She didn't care if she ran into a den of cops. She'd tell them everything. Just like Graham had wanted her to from the start.

She trudged up the hill, not quite at a run but as fast as she could.

As she passed a bush on her left, a hand stretched out from its depths and yanked her into the shadows.

Before she could react, that hand clasped over her mouth, pinning her against a man's chest. She flailed against him, until she felt a wet nose nuzzle her cheek.

Her eyes widened. Emmy.

Which meant...

"Shh," Graham said in her ear. "Don't scream."

He wrapped his warmth around her as another police car raced up the street to the same place the others had stopped: Graham's condo.

EIGHT

The last thing Graham had expected was for Layla to appear, running toward a condo that was swarming with the police who wanted to take her in.

After investigating the alleyway without any leads, he had needed to regroup and come up with a plan. He'd headed to his condo to grab his motorbike before he started his search, but the police had beat him to his door.

Someone probably tipped them off that he'd been spotted with a suspect earlier at the ski resort. It wouldn't help if that someone had identified him as the person who'd ridden the snowmobile onto the slope.

The reason didn't matter, because his place was now filled with officers.

He'd hidden in the bushes, recalibrating his next move, when he heard Layla running up the street.

Relief crashed into him as he wrapped his arms around her shivering body. "Layla, what happened? Where've you been?"

"Why are the police surrounding your condo?"

she whispered through chattering teeth. From cold or from panic, he wasn't sure.

She needed to know she was a suspect in a crime against Flint, but he couldn't tell her here. First, he needed them to get someplace warm to hide. And he needed to know what happened in the alleyway.

He reached over to grip her hand but she winced. His gaze dropped to see her wrists bound. Beneath the zip tie, blood streaked her skin.

Heat simmered up his spine as his jaw clenched tight enough to cause it to throb. Whoever did this to her would pay. Somehow.

He whipped his pack off his back and pulled out his knife. "They hurt you."

She flinched as he cut the band off. "Not as much as they could've."

He pulled out his first-aid kit. "What happened?"

She ducked her head.

He sounded angry. He knew it, but his blood boiled so hot he wanted to slam into something.

He inhaled deeply to steady his tone. "Please, tell me."

She licked her lips. "They surrounded me, threatened to shoot Emmy if I didn't get in the trunk."

Another surge vibrated through his arms. It took all his self-control to steady his hands as he smeared ointment on her wounds.

Twice now, he'd left her alone for a little bit, and twice she'd been abducted. He felt like he was going to be sick. "How did you get away?"

She blew out a shuddering breath as he finished

wrapping her wrists. "He swerved to avoid a deer and landed in a berm." She grimaced. "I Maced him and ran."

Graham opened his mouth to respond, but a voice called out from the condo building.

Now was not the time; they needed to talk later. Their hiding spot would be discovered soon.

He glanced at the street, but Layla's voice broke into his thoughts. "Why are the police here?"

His eyes slid closed. No, not now. He couldn't tell her after what she'd just been through.

"Graham?"

He sighed. "Turns out that someone broke into Flint's office."

Layla curled into Emmy. "Meaning, they are looking for me."

Another round of sirens blared beyond the corner. Emmy sat ramrod straight, probably torn between running to the emergency and comforting Layla.

Graham shrugged his pack back onto his shoulders. "We'll talk about it later. First, we need someplace warm."

Tears gleamed in Layla's eyes, but her mouth twitched into a small smile. "I bet you regret not sending me on my way when you had your chance."

"Not even close." On hands and knees, he peeked around the bush and up the hill toward his condo complex.

Their timing had to be perfect. Two people and a large black Lab wouldn't blend in well.

"I'm so sorry."

He'd almost missed her words, she'd said them so softly. "This isn't your fault."

Her dry laugh sounded like it was dangling off the edge of a sob. "You mean the fact that you're now implicated in this mess has nothing to do with me?"

He didn't answer her question. Just scanned the street. "This is only a setback. I'll fix it."

"How?"

Graham's throat tightened. "If only I'd found Ollie's phone. It contains all the evidence we need."

There it was again—the instinct he was missing something. A piece of the puzzle.

"It still leaves us with nothing."

Her statement, spoken so gently, pulled his gaze back to her. The vulnerability shadowing her face constricted his breath. It reminded him of what would happen if he lost.

He blinked. Hard. No, he couldn't let his mind wander there. He wouldn't let that happen.

The rising moon reflected in her watery eyes. "Graham, some things you can't fix."

A dark foreboding hung in his gut.

His mom had said those very words right before she'd left him, standing alone, waiting for her to pick him up after school. Ollie had said those words, too, when Graham had pried into why he'd been so edgy. The day before he'd been killed.

He clenched his fists. Not again. "We won't let a

man like Flint keep murdering and framing people when he feels like it."

"What if we lose?" Her words floated on her trembling breath.

Graham returned his attention to the street. They didn't have time to discuss this. "I'll figure it out. Once we get you someplace warm."

Two officers walked out of his building, scanning the area. It wouldn't be long before they expanded the perimeter, searching the streets. Now was their chance.

But to where?

The only person he trusted was his fellow ski patroller Jim Simmons. He didn't live too far either. Only about half a mile downhill in the next neighborhood. They might be able to make it there undetected.

Graham looked back at Layla. Her face was pale and drawn, her eyes red rimmed with uncertainty. Or exhaustion. Probably both.

He wrapped his arms around her shoulders. "Okay, we are going to Jim's house. It's not too far from here."

Her exhale sent a cloud into the air. "Are you sure we can trust Jim?"

"There aren't many I trust, but Jim is one of them."

She didn't respond as he helped her stand.

They stepped out of the hedge's shadow, Emmy at their heels, exposed and vulnerable beneath the rising moon's iridescent light. Its reflection cast a lavender glow onto the snow, but clouds began to roll over the moon. Another storm coming in. Graham could feel it in his bones.

Layla leaned heavily into his arms as he moved toward Jim's. Every step echoed in the silence of the quiet neighborhood.

His ears rang as he listened for any footfalls that might be following.

Wait, did he hear something?

He glanced over his shoulder. Nothing, but the hairs on the back of his neck lifted.

He must be going out of his mind. Still, he hurried their pace, with Layla struggling to keep up next to him.

Graham had never been so relieved to see Jim's evergreen A-framed home, with its antique pair of skis hanging below the upper window in an X.

With his arm around Layla, he moved to the front door and knocked.

Footsteps thumped behind the door. A pause. Then Jim opened it, confusion scrunching his face.

"We need a place to hide."

Jim blinked and turned his attention to Layla.

His eyebrows shot up. He stared at Layla, something indiscernible on his face. Something that weaseled into Graham's stomach, making him queasy.

But being on the run must be playing with Graham's mind, because Jim's face relaxed, a smile tugging up on the corner of his mouth. "Of course. Come on in."

* * *

Layla had been safer when she'd hidden alone. In the two years she'd been running from Flint, not once had she been kidnapped. Now she'd been taken twice. How could she have been so foolish to think she could sweep in and out of Silver Ridge without Flint noticing?

Layla's heart rate wouldn't ease. Even after a hot shower and a cup of cocoa nestled between her hands, her insides wouldn't stop shivering. A deep chill that wouldn't let go.

At least Jim's house protected them from the falling snow. The glow of the fire from the stone fireplace elongated her shadow on the white living room walls, which were trimmed in light pine baseboards. She sat on the brown sofa, which probably hid bachelor pad dirt, but at least it was comfortable.

It all gave off the illusion of safety.

She sat alone, her wrists stinging. Graham took a shower while Jim had been called away to his mom's house. If someone chose that moment to barge through the door, what were her chances of escaping a third time?

Each time only fueled Flint's desperation. Desperate enough to frame her for stealing from his office.

The stakes had risen too high. Why did Graham have to get involved at all? He should've left her while he'd had the chance. Didn't he understand that she wasn't worth fighting for? Losing his life for?

Although, thinking back, she never would've made it to the skier's hut without him in the storm. Or made it off the mountain safely. Or escaped the gunman on the snowmobile.

Still, her best bet was to get out of Silver Ridge. Alone. Without Graham. Then maybe Flint would leave him be.

She swallowed, the lump in her throat painful.

Graham stepped into the living room, and her breath hitched.

Wow, the guy cleaned up nice. Better than she remembered.

His wet hair—more red than blond—framed his face. His broad shoulders filled out his evergreen sweater, bringing out his rich brown eyes, which squinted as he smiled at her. A smile that caused her stomach to flutter.

She raised her mug to her lips. Was Graham allowed to look so good when hiding from a killer?

Graham picked up his cell from the end table where he'd plugged it into the wall to charge only an hour ago. "Only thirty percent. I guess the battery was completely drained."

He lowered himself onto the couch and picked up his glass of water from the scuffed coffee table. "Where's Jim?"

Layla fiddled with her mug's handle, trying to ignore the butterflies in her stomach. "He, um, he had a phone call from his mom. I guess she can't get her DVD player to work or something like that, so he said he'd be right back. I guess that means she lives nearby."

"About ten minutes away. She calls often. She's been battling cancer, and he will bend over backwards to help her. I told you he was a good guy."

She tried to smile. Of course Graham was right. So why couldn't she shake this odd foreboding?

She probably imagined it. Being on the run had a way of making her too suspicious. It would be better if she changed the subject. Such as telling Graham she was leaving Silver Ridge. Without him.

Maybe later. Sitting here, with him, soothed something inside. She wanted to savor it just a moment longer.

She took a sip of her hot cocoa, its warmth simmering through her.

He set down his glass of water. "I've been working on a plan on what to do. I don't want to put Jim out for too long."

She had a plan. The right one. He'd even opened the conversation for her to tell him, but the words stuck in her throat.

"Hey, you okay?" The richness of Graham's voice warmed her more than the hot cocoa.

She smoothed her thumb over her mug's handle. "Yeah, I was just thinking—" A pop from the log in the fireplace interrupted.

Graham's eyes softened. "About Ollie?"

No, but now she was. And it gripped her heart and wouldn't let go.

He nodded and leaned forward with his elbows on his knees. "I think about him all the time."

Her chest swelled. "I've been so lonely without him." If anyone understood what it was like to lose Ollie, to lose a brother, Graham would.

He reached over and took her hand, his warmth a healing balm. "Me too."

She inhaled. "Sometimes, over the past two years, I'd put on my fluffiest sweats and huddle under a blanket on the couch wherever I was—a hotel, an apartment, it didn't matter. I'd pretend that I was home. I'd turn on the TV and imagine Ollie with me. I'd even talk to him sometimes."

"You probably had to do most of the talking."

She smiled. "It was a little one-sided. It was embarrassing when my landlord walked in on the conversation. I think she thought I was a little weird."

"I wouldn't doubt it."

She twisted the mug in her hands. "You know, Ollie offered me the first place I ever truly felt at home. My parents—I know they love me, but they never had time to bother with me."

Graham scoffed. "Tell me about it."

Layla watched the fire's glow reflect on Graham's face. "What do you mean?"

Graham sighed. "Let's just say I know a little about uncaring parents. Because of it, I was a bit wayward until I met Ollie. Somehow, he saw my wounds and taught me that Jesus could heal them."

Layla's eyes misted. "Yeah. Me too. I'll never forget the day he came home, and I had packed a bag to run away. I was seventeen and didn't feel like I belonged."

Graham nodded like he knew exactly what she was talking about.

"He said he had an errand that he needed my help with. Somehow, he convinced me to get in the car and drive to a little farm not far from here. I got out of the car, and suddenly five of the cutest little puppies came racing toward us. Only about eight weeks old. Three black ones and two yellow ones. Oh, they were so cute."

She reached down to where Emmy lay at her feet and scratched her ears.

"Then Ollie said to pick one out. I couldn't believe it. I really got to pick out a puppy. I'd asked my parents for years to get a dog, and they would never allow one. I picked up the black one that seemed to want to follow me wherever I went. I named her Emmy."

Graham glanced down at Emmy. "Good choice."

A small laugh escaped Layla. "I'll never forget what Ollie said. He said, 'You belong here, Layla. In Silver Ridge. I need you to help me train Emmy. Prepare her. Because someday, she's going to save lives.'"

"And she has."

Layla brushed away a stray tear rolling down her cheek. "Emmy isn't just any dog. Emmy gave me a reason to stay. A reason to trust."

Which made it impossible to think of leaving without her again. How could she do it? How could she keep running when all she wanted was to snuggle into her brother's bungalow they'd shared, with Emmy at her feet? But those days were gone.

Graham squeezed her hand. "Layla, I know it feels impossible, but don't give up on me. Don't give up on yourself. We'll figure a way out of this. I promise."

Layla's jaw tightened. "You can't promise anything. The law isn't even on our side. The only way we can is if I go out on my own."

Graham scooted closer, his face intense. "That isn't true. The only way to survive is to stick together. Give me a chance, Layla."

More tears started to roll down her face. Graham reached up and brushed them away. "Let me fix this."

She shook her head. "No. What if you can't? What if you get killed?"

"Layla, some things are worth fighting for."

His words struck her breathless. No one had ever thought she was worth fighting for. Not even her parents. She was simply a girl from Denver who got into trouble. But sitting here, the firelight flickering over his face, she almost believed him. Believed that he really did care enough to fight for her.

The thought surged a new warmth deep inside that calmed the trembling.

When had Graham become more than her rescuer? She couldn't quite describe what he'd become, but still—it was something.

Graham was quiet, but he hadn't removed his

hand from her cheek. And with the way he was looking at her, she didn't want to move.

"Layla."

Her whispered name, spoken softly, soothed all the open wounds in her heart like a salve. For so long, she had not heard her name uttered on anyone's lips. But here, in front of the fire, hearing her name, she knew she could never leave. Not if she didn't want to kill her heart, her own humanness, completely.

He leaned in a little. Was he going to kiss her? She sucked in a breath.

The bang of the front door slamming against the wall vibrated through the room. Layla jumped to her feet, her hot cocoa sloshing over the sides, spilling down the front of her flannel.

Her head demanded she run, hide, but her feet wouldn't budge from their spot. Graham, who had fallen into her suddenly vacated cushion, looked up at the front door.

"Well," Jim said standing in the doorway, "don't I have impeccable timing."

A gush of air rushed out of her lungs. She looked at Graham, but instead of anger, a smile slid across his face.

He shrugged. "That is not the word I would use, Jim. *Bad. Bad* is a much better word."

Jim laughed and wandered toward the kitchen.

Graham shook his head as he reached for her hand and guided her back to the seat next to him. He didn't try to kiss her again, simply put his arm around her and flipped on the TV with the remote to the movie *The Goonies*.

Beside her, Graham chuckled at something. How could this—sitting next to him—feel like home?

But it did.

And she couldn't leave. Not with so much to lose.

Now she simply needed to figure out how to keep either of them from being killed.

NINE

The rising sun shone through Jim's kitchen window, leaving a long streak across the floor from the sink to the fridge. Last night's snow had already moved out of the area, leaving behind only a couple of fresh inches.

Graham pushed around the eggs he had made for himself on his plate. Sure, they tasted good, but his mind kept wandering toward Layla. Being close to her last night as they watched a movie, laughing with her, it stirred something new. Something deeper than friendship.

Had he really almost kissed her? Not smart. He should be grateful for Jim's interruption. Yet he wasn't. He couldn't help but wonder what it would've been like.

His eyes squeezed shut. He really needed to get his head back on straight.

The clang of Jim putting his plate in the sink startled Graham back to reality. "So, what are you going to do next?"

"Uh…" Graham blinked hard and exchanged his

fork for his coffee. "I think I need to go ask Zane some questions."

Jim froze. "Zane? Why?"

"I think he knows something."

Jim finished pouring a glass of milk before he said, "Not likely."

Something in Jim's tone made Graham's mug pause halfway to his mouth, but Jim continued on with putting his plate in the dishwasher as if nothing was amiss.

Graham blew it off and set down his mug. "I'm going to go ask, anyway. Can Layla hang here while I'm gone? The last two times I left her, she was taken. I don't want her to be alone."

Jim shrugged, his gaze focused on the dishes in the dishwasher. "Yeah, sure. As long as you don't mind she stays here when I leave for my shift in a little more than an hour."

Uncertainty tightened in Graham's gut. He didn't want Layla left alone. Yet, he really needed to talk with Zane. Two people with a black Lab would be easier to recognize than if he went on his own.

Besides, no one else knew she was here. Here, she'd be out of sight.

He fiddled with the handle of his mug. Wow, he hoped this was the right thing. "That should be fine. Just don't tell anyone that she's here."

A strange expression rolled over Jim's face. "Sure thing."

"Good morning."

Layla appeared in the kitchen door, a smile on her face, her hair hanging around her face in waves.

Graham's heart stuttered to a stop.

Her cheeks turned a slight shade of pink.

She broke eye contact as she moved her hair behind her ear. "Are there any eggs left?"

Jim slid a plate of eggs onto the table. "Your breakfast, madam. Now, if you will excuse me, I have to go do some chores before shift. Some of us have to work for a living. I can't slack off like you do, Graham."

Graham blinked hard. "Speaking of, can you please—"

"Yeah, yeah, I'll cover for you." Jim strode out of the kitchen.

The room fell silent, except for Layla's fork scraping against her plate.

Graham cleared his throat. "Listen, Layla, we need a plan before I leave."

Her eyes swung to his. "Before *you* leave? I'm leaving with you, aren't I?"

He reached out and laid his hand on hers. "I won't be gone long. You'll be safer here."

She snatched her hand away, her gaze sharp. "You weren't gone long when you went for wood at the cabin. Or when you went to talk to your friend at the station. Both times, something happened, Graham."

"Listen—"

"No, *you* listen. This is my fight. If anything, you

are staying here while I… Well, I…don't know. But you aren't leaving without me."

"Layla, here, you'll be out of sight. No one knows you are here. You'll be safer at Jim's."

Her back straightened. "I've done fine on my own for the past two years."

This was ridiculous. Graham stood. "I'll be back as soon as I can. Promise me that you will be here when I do."

She stood, too, with a shrug.

"I'm serious, Layla."

"So am I. I was safer before I came back to Silver Ridge. I need to disappear again. This time for good."

A low rumble escaped Graham's throat. "No, you can't do that. I can't lose you like I lost Ollie. Like I lost—"

He stopped. How had this conversation led back to his mom?

"Like who, Graham?"

He'd done so well stuffing away his memories, but in a single breath, Layla had dug them back out.

Graham crossed his arms. "You're staying here."

Layla folded her arms. "Why are you so determined to rescue me? To keep me here? Does it have anything to do with your mom?"

He rubbed the back of his neck. Why did she have to ask him that?

He'd never really talked with anyone about his mom. Reopening past scars only made the pain, the abandonment, resurface.

She crossed over to him. "Why can't I know about you, Graham? You know almost everything about me."

Gazing into her face, he saw something raw that matched a yearning buried in his own heart.

What was this growing between them? He couldn't say why, but he kind of wanted her to know.

He released a pent-up sigh. "My mom raised me, never knew my dad. She bounced from boyfriend to boyfriend. I always tried to earn her attention. I worked harder in school. Tried keeping the apartment spotless. Tried to fix whatever was broken. It was never enough."

Layla frowned like she knew that feeling. Understood it on a deep level.

He swallowed. "One night, she told me, 'Stop trying so hard. I'm one of those things you just can't fix.' The next day, she dropped me off at school, and I never saw her again. The school called my grandma, and I went to live with her."

Somehow, speaking the words released a constriction in his chest.

Layla's fingers twined through his. "Her loss, Graham."

The corner of his mouth twitched. "Yeah, well, thanks."

"No, I'm serious. Look at you. You save lives, rescuing people in danger on the ski slopes. People like me. Not to mention, you're probably the best skier I've ever met."

Graham stopped trying to hold his smile back. "I'm not sure how important that was to my mom."

"She was the one not good enough for you."

Graham looked down, meeting her sincere gray eyes.

Was he, though? Was he good enough for Layla?

Yeah, he probably wasn't, but he wanted to be.

"I'm sorry, Graham. You deserved more."

The warmth of her hand made him almost believe it. "Thanks."

She drew in a breath as if she wanted to say more but didn't know if she should. She swallowed. "So, what's your plan?"

Somehow, he didn't think that was what she wanted to say. He blinked as if waking from a dream. "I need to find out what Zane knows. It might help us figure out how to expose Flint. At least get him off your trail."

After a final squeeze of his hand, she began to gather the dishes on the table. "Great. I'll just tidy up, then we can go—"

"Layla—"

She stopped, the plate hovering over the dishwasher. "You still don't want me to go."

He took the plate from her and finished putting it in the dishwasher. "Two people with a black Lab are easier to spot than if I go alone. Stay out of sight. Don't forget that the police are looking for you."

"But I might have insight into what Zane says."

"And I'll tell you everything he tells me. I just need you to stay here. Let me keep you safe."

A heavy sigh escaped her. "Fine. You'd better hurry back."

After a lingering look, he slipped on Jim's spare brown coat and black beanie, tucking his hair completely underneath. Then he grabbed his fully charged cell.

On his way out the door, he turned toward her. "Jim is just outside. He'll be around for another hour or so if you need anything. I'll be back as soon as I can."

He studied her, his stomach clenched. Was he doing the right thing?

She finally nodded.

This had to be right. The fewer people who might recognize her, the better.

The town was quiet as he walked toward Zane's house, quickly enough to get there fast, but not so quickly that he drew attention. Zane usually took Sundays off. Graham hoped that this Sunday would be no different.

At the end of the block, he saw Zane's bungalow, its blue siding contrasting with the hardened snowdrifts surrounding its porch.

His cell vibrated in his pocket. He slowed. Who would be calling him? Layla didn't have a cell. Unless she'd borrowed Jim's.

He slipped the phone from his pocket and looked at the screen.

His heart slammed to a stop. The ice-crusted

sidewalk beneath him began to swirl. Almost losing balance, he caught himself with his hand against a nearby tree.

The caller ID read *Ollie*.

He gulped before his thumb swiped across the screen to answer.

His breath hitched. "Ollie?"

Layla heard her own confusion in Graham's "Ollie?" The type of confusion from waking within a nightmare, teetering on the edge of panic.

Ollie's phone. Here in Jim's house. It didn't make sense.

"It's me."

A rush of breath filled the receiver. "Layla?"

"Yeah."

"What? How? Where are you?" Each question picked up with speed, as if his mouth was trying to keep up with his thoughts.

Layla couldn't form words. The few answers she did know would only bring more confusion.

If she hadn't been so curious, she would have left the phone tucked between the T-shirts and the side of the drawer. She would have left it alone, except it was red, her brother's favorite color. Almost like it called to her, but then that would mean she must be losing her mind.

The slick phone almost slipped through her weak fingers, but she forced a tighter grip and turned it on. The battery hadn't even been dead, and the lock screen appeared—a picture of her with a baby Emmy snuggled in her arms.

Her chest had constricted when she saw the picture, unable to breathe.

The password was Emmy's birthday, March 26—0326. No one memorized a dog's birthday except the owner.

Why would Jim have Ollie's cell phone? And why wouldn't he have turned it in if it contained evidence? Or destroyed it?

She leaned against the dresser, a cold sweat prickling her forehead. In all her efforts to stay safe, to stay alive, had she walked right into the lair of the one she'd been trying to avoid?

The battery level hovered at only eight percent. Only enough power to check the pictures. Or call Graham. Not enough for both. Maybe she should've checked the phone's pictures first, but she had to tell Graham. He needed to know that his buddy had had Ollie's phone this entire time. Then maybe he would tell her what to do next.

"Layla? Where are you?" He emphasized his words, a pointed staccato demanding an answer.

"I'm at Jim's."

A beat of silence. "Where is Jim?"

Layla tiptoed to the door of the bedroom and heard running water from the kitchen. "Still in the kitchen. He's almost ready to head to work. I think."

Another beat before he said, "Where are you?"

His question sounded different this time. She detected a hint of desperation to know she was safe. At least, that was what she hoped she heard. "I'm in his room, grabbing some socks."

More silence. "In…his…room? Socks?"

"Yeah, I asked him if I could grab some warmer socks. That's how I found Ollie's phone. I looked in the wrong drawer. There isn't much power left."

Graham's breath shuddered. "Why would Jim have Ollie's cell? He knew I've been looking for it. He even went out there a couple of times helping me look for it."

"Maybe that's how he got it."

A heavy pause lingered on the other end. "He found it first. That was why he wanted to help. He knew something was on that phone."

Which meant Jim wasn't the man Graham had believed him to be. The realization stretched tension over the line.

Her breath came in gasps. "What do I do, Graham? Is Jim working with Flint?"

"Shh. Keep your voice down. He can't know what you found."

"I know, sorry," she whispered, with a glance toward the door. She heard water running from the kitchen.

Heat flushed her cheeks. Had it been Jim who had done Flint's dirty work, had killed her brother? What was Jim capable of?

Defiant tears filled her eyes. She couldn't grieve now. She needed to toughen up. Get to the bottom of why Jim had Ollie's phone. Figure out the truth.

The tremor in her stomach quickened. "What do I do?"

"Get out of there." Graham's voice sounded low and intense, sending a tremor to her fingers. "Wait until he leaves for work and meet me by the Victor trailhead west of the skating rink. That trail goes over Howard Pass back toward Fairplay. Bring the phone with you. I think that's the key to proving Flint is a murderer."

Layla brought a shaky hand to her forehead. "Okay."

"Layla, listen to me. The game has changed. That phone could be the key to your freedom. We just need to get it to the authorities. If that phone contains what I think it does, it could be the evidence needed to prove your story."

A swell of something new seeded within her gut. The game had indeed changed, and for the first time, she was the one holding the good cards.

"I'm going to have a chat with Zane, then I'm coming straight to you. Promise you won't take off without me."

Layla glanced down at Emmy lying beside her. The man fought hard for answers. Not for his own sake, but for hers. Could it be that he found her worth it?

She soaked in the realization, a sense of awe settling over her. Maybe together, they were stronger. Maybe together, they could keep each other safe.

Maybe it was time to show Graham that she wasn't going anywhere without him.

"Yes," she said, her voice soft, "I promise. As soon as Jim leaves, I will meet you there."

"Good." His sigh fluttered through the receiver. "And, Layla, don't forget—"

The phone died.

Her mind flipped through all the possible endings to his sentence. Don't forget what?

She squeezed the phone. She needed to charge it on the cable Graham had used last night out in the living room, then send the pictures to Graham before anything happened to it.

She crept out of Jim's room and surveyed the living room. The power cable lay across the end table, right where Graham had left it the night before. How could she charge the phone without Jim noticing?

She reached for the cable.

"I put a stew in the Crock-Pot." Jim walked into the room, wiping his hands on a towel. Layla straightened so fast her head spun. She swung the phone behind her back and slumped, taking on a casual stance.

Jim smiled, but something in his eyes looked different. Maybe even cold. "Hope that sounds good for dinner. Ain't fancy, but it's Graham's recipe."

Her smile twitched, but she held it steady. "I'm sure it'll be great."

He stepped closer, and the room became smaller. "You found those socks?"

"Yep." She held her foot up to prove it.

He nodded but didn't move. Simply stood, watching her. As if he could read the guilt lining her face.

He swung his arm toward the couch. "Sit. Relax. I want you to feel at home here."

With as little movement as possible, she slipped the phone into her back pocket, then moved over to the couch. "Thank you. You've been so kind."

She picked up the ski magazine on the coffee table and crossed her legs, but Jim hadn't budged. He just stood there, looking at her.

What was he doing?

She peeked down at her watch. Only a few minutes and then he would head off to work. All she had to do was act like nothing had changed.

She smiled again.

He smiled back, still not moving.

"So, um, you really don't have to stick around on my account. I mean, I know you need to get to the slopes. I'll be fine. I'm sure."

He folded his arms. His smile now looked like plastic, like he was forcing it out instead of a sneer. "I decided to take the day off. I mean, your safety is important."

A cold sensation iced down her veins. He knew. She didn't know how, but somehow he knew. "Please don't adjust your schedule for my sake. I'll be fine. The only one who knows I'm here is Graham." She swallowed. "And you."

He sat in the recliner, his arms folded. "Nah, I had some time built up. I can afford to lose a day."

Her spine stiffened. The pulse in her ears shouted

that she had to get out of here. "Sounds great. I won't be so lonely, then. Excuse me, I just need to go to the bathroom."

She stood and reined in her reflexes to a slow saunter, but she closed the door with too much force.

She winced as she locked the door. Rubbing her hands, she paced the full length of the bathroom. They should've known Jim would catch on. It was like he could read her face.

She inhaled, trying to calm her huffs. She needed to breathe. Needed to think.

Her eyes flitted around the bathroom. She looked up.

A window. Perfect.

After a glance toward the door, listening for any sound from the living room, she reached up and unlocked the window. It opened without making a noise.

She hesitated. What about Emmy? How could she take her along without alarming Jim?

No, it was her and Graham in danger. Jim wouldn't hurt Emmy. She didn't think. Once she met up with Graham, they could return together to get her dog.

With her mind made up, she flushed the toilet. While the whirl of water sounded in the room, she pulled herself up onto the sink in a crouching position. She turned on the faucet, its rush hiding any noise as she removed the screen and lowered it to the ground.

Without bothering to turn off the water, she

slipped through the window. It wouldn't take long for Jim to realize she had escaped. She would have only a couple of minutes to disappear. Somehow, she would have to hide her footprints.

Using her upper body, she delicately lowered herself to the snow-covered ground below the window.

She whipped around, only to barrel into a hardened chest.

The wind was knocked out of her as she bounced away, but Jim's hands wrapped tightly around her arms, keeping her from falling backward. She pressed her palms against his chest, pushing away, but he only squeezed tighter, not allowing her to breathe.

He lowered his hand. She froze as he pulled Ollie's phone from her back pocket.

He let go, and she shoved away from him. He held the phone between his thumb and index finger, dangling it in front of her.

She grunted as she reached to grab it. He pulled it away, a wicked sneer taking over his face.

"Now, I wonder what you want with this."

A yell built in her chest as she lunged for the phone again. He held it up above her head, out of her reach.

"Why are you doing this, Jim? You must know this is wrong."

He looked at the phone, his face conflicted. Maybe she could get through to him.

"Come on. You're one of Graham's friends. You were Ollie's friend too. Why don't you help us?"

For a brief moment, his brow lowered with indecision. She held her breath, waiting for him to choose good.

She straightened her shoulders. "Why did you keep it these past three weeks since Ollie's death if not because you knew handing it to Flint was wrong?"

He raised a single eyebrow without a word, and she knew she'd lost.

He shrugged. "Leverage. Now I have no choice but to make *you* my leverage."

With the form of a major-league pitcher, he wound back his arm and hurled the phone into a nearby rock.

She watched it shatter. Along with her hope.

TEN

Graham's chest was clenched tight, and he struggled to inhale. Ollie's phone. The phone he'd searched for through feet of snow, risking avalanche danger, had been at Jim's all along.

How could he be such a fool? Once again, his trust had been shredded. It only proved the one person he could trust was himself.

He turned toward Jim's house, ready to interrogate his old bud. The double-crossing…

But he stopped. No matter how much his hand burned to hold Ollie's phone, to see the pictures that had led to his friend's murder, he couldn't return. Not without causing suspicion.

Jim would wonder why he had returned so soon. Maybe even start to ask questions. They could not let Jim know they'd found the phone. Jim needed to believe everything was normal. Otherwise, the element of surprise may be ruined.

He squeezed his own cell phone in his grip, struggling to focus. He needed to be cool. Calculated.

Would the pictures on Ollie's phone be enough

evidence to convince Deputy Dillinger of Layla's innocence?

Maybe, but the more information, the better. Between whatever was on that cell phone, and the information he might get from Zane, it could make a much stronger case to convince Dillinger that Layla was the victim.

He shoved his hands deep into his pockets and forced his feet up the steps of Zane's porch.

The doorbell resounded inside as a gust of wind pelted the home's siding.

Zane answered the door in gray sweats and a black patrol hoody. Instead of his dark hair being combed back like usual, it hung over his forehead. He didn't say anything. Instead, his eyes scoped out the street behind Graham.

Graham didn't have time for small talk. "Zane, I want answers. I know—"

"Shush or you will get us both killed," Zane said beneath his breath, his lips barely moving.

He ushered Graham in, then closed the door and locked it.

"I'm not here for a visit, Zane. I need—"

"I know." Zane rushed around the living room, closing the curtains.

After he'd finished, he stood in front of Graham with his arms crossed. "Now we can talk, but you have to keep your voice down. The neighbors can't know you are here."

Three days ago, Graham would have called Zane

paranoid. Now it only reaffirmed that Zane knew something. "What's going on?"

Zane's jaw twitched before he shook his head. "I can't tell you."

"What do you mean, you can't tell me? I spent a night up in Lone Man's Hut after running from a gunman, only to be chased down the next day by a snowmobile. Plus, cops are crawling all over my place, and you say that you can't tell me what is going on?"

Zane rubbed a hand over his eyes. "I know it hasn't been easy for you—"

"Hasn't been easy? When is the last time you've had to outrun a gunman?"

Zane scratched the stubble along his jawline. A motion that indicated it might have been more recent than Graham had assumed.

He wasn't going to get Zane to crack by acting like a scared twerp. He inhaled. "Okay, fine, look, there are some shady things happening in this town. Shady things like the DA getting away with murder. I don't really care about all of that. What I care about is Layla. This guy is after her, determined to shut her up. She's been nearly kidnapped twice."

Zane's eyes widened.

"She doesn't deserve this. All I want is information to stop him. One less bad guy in this town. Isn't that enough reason to tell me something, anything, that might help me?"

Zane folded his arms across his chest. "Tell me

about Layla Quin. Where has she been, and why is she back?"

"No, sir, I'm asking the questions. You knew something was up when she said her name. Why?"

"Again, I can't tell you."

A growl balled up in Graham's stomach. Wow, he wanted to yell, but Zane was right. No reason to alert the neighbors. Instead, he brought his voice down to a lethal level. "I'm trying to save her life. Cameron Flint is one powerful dude. If he has committed murder, what else is he getting away with? We can stop him."

Zane glanced around the room. "This goes a whole lot deeper than Cameron Flint."

The heaviness of Zane's statement settled on Graham's shoulders. If the DA was just the start, how far did the corruption go? "Someone has Flint in their back pocket?"

Zane gave one nod, almost unnoticeable. "If I say more, it could blow everything."

Everything? "Who are you?"

"Nobody important. Just a guy who wants to see justice."

Maybe he and Zane weren't so different after all. The burn to see justice ignited in his gut, and it matched the lines of determination etching Zane's face. "If we can expose Flint, wouldn't that leave whoever is at the top more vulnerable?"

Zane's eyes narrowed. "Maybe, but I cannot let anyone know I'm onto them. If they figure out who I really am, my plan will not work."

Who he really is?

A chill ran down Graham's arms. Maybe he had Zane figured out all wrong. "Then leave Flint to me. I work better alone, anyway."

"So I've noticed."

"What can you tell me about Flint?"

Zane didn't speak. He stepped backward, then turned toward the kitchen. Graham followed him in.

The kitchen had probably been renovated in the 90s, its white appliances scuffed with use. The white laminate countertops were at least clean and contrasted against the dark brown cabinets.

Zane poured himself a cup of coffee. He then held up the carafe, offering some to Graham, but Graham shook his head.

Zane returned the carafe and motioned for Graham to sit at the small wooden table for two in the center of the room.

Graham thought he might explode. Why wouldn't the guy simply come out with it?

Finally, Zane sat across from him, his gaze intense. "Okay, look, Flint has most of the cops under his control."

"Yeah, I figured that out when I tried to talk with Deputy Dillinger and found out Flint was accusing Layla of raiding his office."

Zane tapped the table with his index finger. "Deputy Dillinger is the only one who I might— *might*—trust. I've asked him a couple of questions, and the answers he has given me make me suspect he is very skeptical of Flint. Like he has suspicions but can't confirm them."

"Matt has always seemed like on the up-and-up."

"Yeah, well, it's going to take something to pull him over that line to helping us."

Graham examined Zane, trying to discern how much he could trust him. He might have that something, but did he dare share it? The phone, whatever was on it, wouldn't help if he kept it a secret. But who he trusted was key.

The muscle in Zane's jaw ticked. "Look, you are obviously not telling me everything. How about you give me some info, then I give you some info."

"Okay, you start."

"I already did. Now, it's your turn."

Graham studied Zane. An information trade might be the only way he could get anything out of Mr. Spy Man. "Ollie was murdered because of something he saw."

"You've already told me that. Something new. Like why Flint wants Layla dead."

Graham sighed. "Fine. She witnessed…well, let's say criminal activity."

"Are we talking embezzlement or something like murder?"

Graham didn't answer. He wouldn't give away Layla's secrets.

"So murder, then."

"I didn't say that."

Zane lifted an eyebrow. "No, you didn't. If it was, I would say it doesn't surprise me. It wouldn't be the first. But it would be the first that a witness lived to talk about it."

A cold fist squeezed Graham's stomach. "So, you see the desperation of the situation."

Zane leaned forward with his elbows on the table. "You need to get her out of town."

"She can't stay running forever."

"No, but unless you have some irrefutable evidence against Flint, then Flint has the upper hand around here."

"Irrefutable? Like maybe pictures on a phone."

Zane stilled, his eyes locking with Graham's. "Yeah, maybe like some pictures. It depends. What do you have?"

A major piece of Graham begged him to stay quiet, but he heard himself speaking the words before he could stop. "I'm not sure yet, but Layla found Ollie's phone in Jim's house."

Zane's coffee mug paused halfway to his mouth. "The same phone you were looking for? At Jim's house?"

Graham swallowed. "Yep."

Zane set down his mug and folded his arms. "I didn't suspect Jim."

"Me neither," Graham mumbled.

They looked at each other until Zane finally gave a brief nod. Like a silent understanding linked them together.

"Can you get me that phone?"

Graham winced.

"If not me, then Deputy Dillinger. Someone has to see whatever is on it."

"How do I know I can trust either one of you?"

Zane's mouth pinched into a straight line with a long silence. "Because if you don't, then you and Layla are as good as dead." He sighed. "It is likely not enough but worth a try."

Graham ran a hand down his face. Could he rely on Zane? Probably not, but the gravity of the situation didn't leave him any choice. If he trusted him, they could be dead. If he tried to fix it himself, they could be dead. "I'm meeting Layla when we are through here to look at the phone. If I feel like I need to show you the pictures, I'll forward—"

"Don't ever communicate with my phone. They'll use the records against us."

"Fine, I'll somehow leave copies taped beneath Doleman's Bridge on the edge of town."

"Not a good plan, Graham. If those pictures fall into the wrong hands—"

"I'll make sure they remain hidden."

Zane's eyes narrowed. "I still don't like it, but fine. I'll be there at eight in the morning. No later, no sooner, so you better make sure it's there."

"It will be."

"You better go. Someone might be watching the house."

"Fine." Graham stood and started toward the front door.

"Wait."

Graham turned around.

"Go out the back door. Just in case."

Wow. What did this guy know that had him so spooked? "Who are you?"

Zane held his gaze steady, unflinching. "Someone you can trust."

Graham hesitated, locked into Zane's stare. "Good."

He walked toward the back door.

"And, Graham?"

Graham stopped with his hand on the door.

A hint of a desperation glistened in Zane's eyes. "Don't trust anyone. I mean it—no one else."

Graham nodded.

"And also, Graham…" His jaw twitched. "Don't get killed."

Graham's chest knotted up. He forced himself to take a breath before he said, "I don't plan on it."

He stepped into the cold morning air, but it was the ominous warning that chilled him to his core.

Layla blamed the shock of finding Ollie's phone. What else could have caused her to be caught off guard by Jim?

The instincts she'd honed over the last two years, evading and disappearing, must have weakened at the discovery of her brother's phone.

Unless it was hope that had dulled her senses.

The closet walls Jim had locked her in pressed in around her, its darkness only broken by the gap at the bottom of the door. Her legs itched to pace, but the confined space only allowed one step in each direction.

She leaned her head back against the wall. Oh, why hadn't she sent the pictures before she called Graham? Before the phone battery died? A mistake that might mean her end.

If she didn't get out of here soon, the scream balling up in her throat might release, burning up the energy she needed to conserve for her escape. Once she figured out how to escape.

Jim had kept Emmy out in the living room, but Layla could hear her whimpering. The crying ripped at her heart, and she clamped her hands over her ears.

She had to get out of here.

Was Graham already at their meeting spot? Waiting for her?

She had promised him she would be there. If she didn't show up, what would he think?

Graham would most likely presume Jim had left for work, unsuspecting of her discovery. If he believed she had decided to disappear on her own, like she feared he would, he wouldn't look for her.

No one would.

Her breathing sped up. Raw desperation traveled through her arms, and she rattled the doorknob again. No, she didn't think it would suddenly open, but she couldn't just sit and wait for Jim's next move.

Using two hands, she twisted the doorknob, pushing with her shoulder. It didn't even budge.

She smacked her palms against the door. "Come on, Jim. Let me out of here."

No answer. She didn't even know where he was. He may not even be able to hear her.

Emmy did, though. She released two high-pitched barks, trying to answer back. Then, as if something in the room changed Emmy's mood, a low growl rumbled.

"No one can hear you!" Jim shouted back. "My neighbors are nowhere close enough."

"I don't need your neighbors to hear me. Only you. Let me out of here."

"It's your own fault you are in there. If you hadn't snooped, everything would be right as rain."

Except for the fact that he was an accomplice to murder.

She knew she shouldn't ask. He had no reason to answer, but she missed her brother, and by golly, she needed to know. "Jim, what really happened to my brother?"

Silence.

No, she hadn't really expected an answer, but tears sprang to her eyes, anyway.

Ollie's phone had contained the truth. The evidence she needed had been in her hands. The evidence that would've given her testimony credit.

Now it was gone. And Graham would be gone if she couldn't make it to the trailhead.

She couldn't cry. Crying made her weak. Made her less alert. She swallowed back a sob, but it escaped, anyway.

A cell phone trilled in the other room. Jim answered. "Yep?"

Only a beat of silence before he said, "I don't… Was…escape…got it."

Who was he talking to? She pressed her ear to the door and held her breath to eliminate all sound so she could hear.

"You know I don't do that kind of thing… Yeah… I know. Fine, I'll meet you there."

Where? Did that mean he would be leaving? Without giving her any other clues, he hung up.

Layla crouched into the corner of the closet. He would come for her next.

She had two choices: fight the moment he opened the door, which would probably lead to him overpowering her fast, stripping her of any other options. Or she could pretend to be submissive and wait for her chance to escape.

He may be smart enough to know that if she tried to escape once, she'd try again, but maybe being submissive would lull him off his guard.

She straightened and smoothed her hair out of her face. She could be nice. Act like she'd lost the willpower to fight.

Jim opened the closet door, his shadow looming over her.

Yep, trying to overpower him would be a bad plan.

He yanked her out of the closet by her wrists before he twisted her around and tightened a plastic strap around the flaring gashes left from the first time.

She stifled a flinch. Somehow, she had to take the focus away from her fear and engage him in conversation. Making him less vigilant was her only chance of escape.

She swallowed. "Was that Flint on the phone?"

Her voice pitched higher on the last word as Jim tightened the strap.

She closed her eyes. "Why are you doing this? I don't even know you. Don't you think that if I was going to squeal on Flint, I would have done it two years ago?"

Without an answer, he led her by the arm toward the living room.

Emmy squeezed past Jim the moment he opened the door. Pawing Layla's pant leg, she let out a little whimper.

Layla leaned over so Emmy could lick her cheek. "It's okay, girl. It'll be okay."

Jim watched without interfering. Layla may have imagined it, but she thought she saw a streak of compassion cross his face.

She straightened. "Thank you for taking good care of Emmy. For not hurting her."

He grunted.

"And for letting me out of the closet." As if she were the one in the wrong.

His eyebrows drew together. "I'm not a monster."

"I never thought you were."

He led her to a chair and shoved her into it. Without her hands in front to catch herself, her shoulder collided with the end table. Okay, that might've been a little monster-ish. Emmy lay down on her feet.

He picked up a bowl filled with what looked like kibble from near the back door and dropped it beneath Emmy's nose, a few pieces scattering to the floor. "Here, dog. Maybe you'll actually eat now that I let your princess out."

Emmy sniffed the bowl, unsure.

"Eat, dog. You're gonna need your strength."

Emmy looked up at Layla. Layla didn't know what Jim had planned. It would be best if Emmy ate. "Go ahead, girl. It's okay."

It was all the permission Emmy needed, and she began to guzzle down the food.

As if satisfied, Jim went to the coatrack by the front door and put his coat on.

Layla watched, the noise of Emmy's crunching cracking the silence. "Where are you going?"

"You're coming too."

"To where?"

"You'll see."

His tone stirred panic within her gut. "Look, Jim, I know what Flint wants to do with me. He thinks I'll talk. But who will believe me? You destroyed the only possible evidence."

Jim's scowl deepened.

"Why did you save it, anyway? The phone. If you knew the pictures could—"

"It's called saving myself," he snapped. "If I ever

needed a way out, I'd have it. Show them the pictures of Flint killing someone, I'd be offered a plea deal. Now, because of you, I had to destroy it. I couldn't let you ruin everything too soon."

"In other words, you know that Flint can't get away with it forever. He will be caught."

"But not before you are silenced." Jim zipped up his jacket with one swift jerk. "Graham too. Now that he's involved, he'll die, too, and it's all your fault. If you hadn't told him, he would've been just fine."

Her heart clamored into her throat. She couldn't let Graham die because of her mess. She swallowed, trying to keep the panic from trembling in her voice. "I can save him from Flint. Graham will follow me if you let me go. We will disappear, never speaking a word about any of this."

Jim hesitated before his face screwed into a scowl. "If I let that happen, it will be my hide."

"Then somehow fake that you took care of it. Graham and I, we can be very good at playing dead. Take pictures, whatever you think would convince Flint. Then we'll disappear, and you won't have any blood on your hands. And your friend will live."

Jim worked his jaw from side to side. "That would never work. Flint is too smart. Then I'd be a goner too."

Icy fingers wrapped around her throat, trapping any response. What could she say to convince him?

Finishing her meal, Emmy licked her chops, her eyes on Layla.

The only way to save Graham was to escape. She just needed the right opportunity.

Jim gripped her arm and yanked until she stood. "She's done. Let's go."

As she passed the coatrack, Jim tossed her coat over her shoulders, then directed her out the front door toward his Jeep.

Her knees trembled, her legs feeling like jelly. She was running out of time. If she got in that vehicle, she would have no control of where he would take her. The chances of hitting another deer were close to zero. This was her only chance.

He swung the door open for her to get in.

She stopped, her stomach so tight she might be sick. "Jim, if you make me get in there, if you let Flint boss you around, your friend Graham is as good as dead."

The tendon in his neck twitched, but he didn't say anything.

"I know you don't care about me, but I can get Graham away from here safe. Please let me."

Jim's grip on the door shifted, his sporadic gaze jumping from tree to tree, uncertainty twisting his face.

Now was her chance. He may catch her—he was faster—but she would have the element of surprise.

She pretended to start getting into the vehicle, but at the last second, she spun on her heel and took off for the woods.

"Come on, Emmy!" she called, knowing Emmy would follow, but she didn't hear her dog's paws gaining on her.

"Emmy!" She didn't dare look around to see how far Emmy was behind her. It would only slow her down.

"Emmy!"

Still, Emmy didn't respond. Layla glanced over her shoulder.

Emmy was about halfway between her and Jim, who simply leaned against the Jeep door, watching.

Layla's legs slowed to a stop as her attention returned to Emmy.

With her eyes fixed on Layla, Emmy wasn't running. Instead, she staggered forward.

"Come on, Emmy!"

The yearning to obey echoed in Emmy's eyes as she let out a little whimper. She then meandered to the right, then to the left, before she dropped to the ground.

"Emmy!" Layla heard her voice, but it didn't sound like her. It sounded distant. Foreign.

A haze traveled across her eyesight as she fell to her knees beside her friend.

"Emmy?"

Her dog's chest rose and fell, alive, but her eyes remained closed. Not even a twitch in response to Layla's voice.

"What did you do to her?" Layla shouted, her voice raspy.

"She'll be fine. As long as you do what you are told."

Wait. The food. That was why he was so intent on Emmy eating.

"You poisoned her."

Jim watched beneath hooded eyes. "I did what I had to do."

He was using Emmy as a pawn to control her.

Layla leaned over and nestled her cheek into Emmy's soft fur. "Come on, girl. Come back to me."

Layla closed her eyes as her head rose with Emmy's breath. What choice did she have now? For Emmy, she had to follow Jim's orders. She hoped that once Graham discovered she was gone, he would run far from Silver Ridge.

She stood, her knees quaking, but they couldn't give out. Not now. Not when Emmy's life now depended on her.

Without looking at Jim holding open the door, she slid into the back seat.

ELEVEN

This wasn't going to work.

Graham's feet slowed, the rendezvous trail only half a mile away. Not once since Layla had returned had he let the thought free, but now there was no way around it.

He breathed in the frigid air, chilling his lungs and his gung-ho attitude. He hadn't learned much from Zane, but their conversation had revealed one thing. One very important thing he had missed until now.

This was big. Deep. Like, Wonderland deep, with no escape.

His fight wasn't just against a corrupt DA but also an entire system. A system that Zane apparently knew more about.

Zane had not offered any confidence for Layla to be free. In fact, he'd given Graham the impression that they were up against a boa constrictor. The more they fought, the tighter its strangling hold.

Every ounce of fight driving him to free Layla drained, leaving him weak and vulnerable.

He couldn't lose her. If she stayed to fight, only

because he'd told her to, and she lost, he would be the guilty one.

The definition of protection now meant something different. It meant surviving.

And sometimes, to survive, it meant not entering the battle at all.

Maybe hiding was the best thing. For the both of them.

They could go across the country. Assume new names. Get married. He heard that South Carolina was nice. No skiing, but he could get over his urge to hit the slopes.

For Layla, he would give it up.

He moved forward again, his pace quicker than before. New purpose renewed his energy.

It was time to leave Silver Ridge.

He approached the trailhead. The area looked vacant; not many hikers when the temps hovered below thirty and snow iced the trail.

"Layla?" He kept his voice low. He couldn't attract any attention.

No answer.

He went a few steps up the trail, looking around the large trees. He couldn't find a trace of her. The wind stirred the snow into ripples, but there were no footprints. No one had come near the trailhead since before the storm.

Where could she be? She'd had plenty of time to be here by now.

A dark, familiar dread clawed at his stomach.

No. He refused to believe she would abandon

him. He meant something to her. He had felt it in her touch. Seen it in her eyes.

Yet why else would she not be here? If she was going to run off with Ollie's phone and disappear, why had she called him at all?

No, nothing would keep her from meeting him. Not unless—

His pulse pounded in his ears. What if Jim hadn't gone into work? What if he had somehow discovered Layla with Ollie's phone?

The fabric of his coat rustled as he shifted to retrieve his cell. After pulling off his glove with his teeth, his finger trembled as he called Jim.

Within moments, Jim answered. "Hey, bud, what's up?"

Graham analyzed Jim's tone. He sounded normal. "Where is she?"

"Where is who?"

"Layla. She was going to meet me, but she isn't here."

"How would I know? I've been on the slopes."

No, something was off. Jim may sound normal, but Graham couldn't ignore his inner alarm. "Are you lying to me? Where is she?"

He heard Jim exhale over his receiver. "Dude, what's got you so worked up? I haven't seen her since I left for my shift. You told me she'd be fine."

Graham ran his hand down his face. No. This couldn't be happening.

Something clicked over the line, like Jim had

shifted the phone in his hand. "Where are you? Do you need me to come and help look for her?"

Graham paced. *Think. Think.* No ideas came. "Jim, I know you have something to do with all of this. I mean, Layla found Ollie's cell phone at your place."

Jim paused, briefly, but long enough for Graham to notice. "That's crazy, Graham. Ollie's phone was lost. We both know that. What's gotten into you?"

Graham didn't know. Here he stood, accusing his friend of terrible things, yet he didn't know anything. "Layla called from Ollie's phone. She said she found it in your drawer."

"Seriously, Graham, you need your head examined. If Layla called from Ollie's phone…if…then she found it somewhere else. Unless…well…maybe it's been in her possession all along?"

Graham stopped pacing. "What's that supposed to mean?"

"Look, you don't really know where she's been these last couple of years. Maybe she's been working with Flint all along. We already know she dated him. What if she's his pawn to play you? Entrap you. Maybe frame you. I don't know. You've been the one suspicious of Ollie's death."

He had been the *only* one suspicious of Ollie's death, but that didn't mean Layla would come back out of the blue to knock him off the bad guy's trail. Layla was sweet. Kind. Loving. She wouldn't deceive him like that.

Graham clenched his jaw. "You have no idea what you're talking about."

"I'm sorry, man. I don't want to upset you, but seriously, you're so taken with this gal you aren't thinking straight. She came back into town like a ghost, making you promise not to tell anyone about her return."

"Because a powerful man wants to kill her."

"Or because she's helping Flint. Maybe he's the one calling the shots."

This was insane. She wouldn't do that. This was Layla they were talking about. She didn't have a deceitful bone in her body.

Although, she had refused to talk to anyone, committing him to silence. She'd said she didn't want to be discovered. That no one would believe her story. But what if her story was made up? Maybe there was a reason no one ever believed her stories. Maybe they were all incredulous lies.

"Look, man—" Jim's voice sounded sympathetic "—I'm only saying this because I care about you, but what if she was there when Ollie died and that's how she got that phone?"

The trees above Graham rustled in the breeze. The wind was picking up. Graham turned to face it, wishing it would wake him up from this nightmare. "Ollie was her brother. She wouldn't do that."

"A brother that she stopped all communication with for the past two years."

"She was running from a murderer."

"Says her. Not one person can corroborate her

story. Seriously, who are you going to believe? Me, a friend who has been around since high school, or her, who you haven't seen a trace of for the past two years?"

A vibration of static interfered with reception. Not so different from the static sizzling in Graham's head.

"Graham…" Jim's voice became muffled in the static. "Layla is not who she says she is. Trust me."

Graham hated that phrase. *Trust me.* It was a phrase his mom had used. Usually in the same speech about how they were a team. Look how that had turned out. It was a lie.

Don't trust anyone. Zane's words sliced through the static.

Graham held the receiver close to his mouth. "I don't trust anyone."

He punched the end button on his cell and squeezed the phone in his fist.

It didn't compute. Jim painted a picture of not just a deceitful Layla but also a conniving Layla. One who would kill. It contrasted drastically against the Layla he knew. The one who talked about Ollie like he had been not only her brother but also her best friend.

No, he would never believe that Layla had anything to do with Ollie's death. And if Jim lied about that, he would lie about all of it.

Graham reviewed Jim's words. He had sounded so convincing. At least until he'd said one thing: *Maybe she's been working with Flint all along.*

Not once had Flint's name been mentioned in their conversations. He'd purposely left out Flint's name to keep Jim from getting tangled up in the mess.

Graham squeezed his eyes shut. Jim wasn't simply lying to cover himself. He was throwing Graham off the trail.

Why would Jim try so hard to confuse Graham? What did he know?

Unless it wasn't what he knew, but who he wanted to harm.

What if what Jim really wanted was to make Graham believe Layla had ditched him, taking away Graham's reason to search for her.

He drew in shallow breaths.

Another terrifying thought triggered Graham's heart to race. If Jim knew Layla had found the cell, then what would his next step be? What would he do to her?

What did most trapped animals do? They became violent.

Graham hunched over with his hands gripping his knees.

Jim had Layla.

The blindfold over Layla's eyes itched. It smelled like a toolshed mixed with the stench of body odor, intensifying the nausea in her stomach.

Her heart ached as she listened to the lies Jim spewed over the phone. He'd held a gun to her head and said if she uttered a sound, he'd shoot.

No chance to defend herself. No way to counter what was being said about her.

Had Graham believed Jim's lies?

Bile burned the back of her throat. If Graham did believe Jim's lies, which experience told her he would, no one was coming to help. She was all alone once again.

Disorientation had set in a long time ago. At first, she'd tried to keep track of the Jeep's direction, but at this point, they could be anywhere. All she could do was sit with her hands tied behind her back, swaying with every hairpin turn of the Jeep.

Before Jim put the blindfold over her eyes, she saw him lift a large wire crate with Emmy into the cargo area of the Jeep. She called for Emmy, but all she gained was Jim yelling for her to be quiet.

Heat poured over her from the vent. It was getting hot, sweat beads soaking into her blindfold. Her stomach lurched.

"Can you turn down the heat? Please? I think I'm going to be sick."

Jim murmured under his breath, "I should have put tape over your mouth."

Layla swallowed against the bile burning in her throat. What was the use?

Ice from the road pinged the Jeep's undercarriage as it leaned around another curve. The road could be edging along a cliff, for all she knew. One slip of the wheel and she could be dead.

If she was going to survive, it would be up to

her. First, she had to control her queasiness and think clearly.

Jim was taking her to see Flint. That much she knew, but where and when were only a guess.

She couldn't face Flint. Not if she wanted to live. Somehow, she had to get away before they arrived at their destination.

If only the echoes of her heart could travel to that trailhead to reassure Graham of the truth. That Jim had told him lies. That she wanted to keep her promise and meet him there. That she wasn't like his mom. Then maybe—maybe—he would come for her.

Well, she couldn't. And he wouldn't. Which meant she was on her own.

She leaned her head back against the seat, clenching her jaw so tight it ached. Maybe if she could get Jim talking, tell her what he knew, she would find something to use against him.

It wasn't like she could go anywhere…yet.

"So, um…" She swallowed the acid pumping into her throat. "Why are you doing this?"

No answer.

"I mean, you're not a bad guy, Jim. Graham considered you a friend, and he is a good judge of character. What would persuade you to cast your lot in with Flint?"

"I don't know why you are so surprised. Didn't you date him a couple of years ago?"

Ouch. Why did he have to bring that up? "First of

all, that was a long time ago. Second of all, I didn't know he was a criminal—you did."

She heard the sound of leather from the driver's seat, as if Jim had shifted in his seat. "It's a long story."

"And where am I going to go, Jim?"

He clammed up again, probably thinking it unwise to tell her anything.

"Look, who am I going to tell? You are taking me to Flint, aren't you? I'm not too naive to know what he wants to do to me. I just want to know why someone I thought we could trust—or at least someone Graham could trust—would double-cross us."

Layla's body slammed into the front seat as Jim braked. "I didn't double-cross him. He is the one who got in the way. If he had only left Ollie's death alone, stopped investigating, things would be fine. Then you come along and manipulate him into becoming your hero. All of this is your fault."

"I didn't manipulate him to do anything."

"This big-brother responsibility came from somewhere, and it just fanned his determination to find out the truth."

"What is wrong with truth? Huh? If you are so afraid of truth, then maybe you need to get out of whatever trouble you've landed yourself in. People are only afraid of the truth when it will shine a light on what is being done in the dark."

Silence. A silence that carried a tangible weight. The Jeep moved forward again.

Layla let out a long sigh. "What happened to my brother? I just need to know."

The Jeep traveled for several paces before he said, "He took some pictures. I think he was trying to prove your story so that you could come home, but Flint would never allow that. Then he killed him, knowing it would bring you back so he could kill you too. I just wish that you hadn't dragged Graham into it. Now he'll have to die too."

"He doesn't have to. You don't have to go along with this."

Several beats of silence stretched until he finally said, "Yes, I do."

Then Layla remembered. Remembered how he'd rushed out the door to help his mom because she was sick. "This is about your mom. Are you getting money to help your mom?"

He didn't respond. Didn't have to. The core of his actions rested upon someone he loved.

Layla's voice softened. "Jim, there are other ways to help her."

"It's too late. If I backed out, Flint would still destroy you, then me. He has to."

Something in Jim's voice made Layla's breath hitch. "Why would he have to?"

"All you need to worry about is what you'll say to Flint when he sees you."

Layla's chest constricted, her breath coming in gasps. Did this go beyond a corrupt district attorney?

She squeezed her eyes closed. *Oh, God, what do I do?*

She needed to fix this, but never had she felt so helpless. Powerless to stop the pendulum from crushing not just her but also Graham and Emmy.

Only God could help. God wouldn't let such evil prevail, would He?

Jim was right: this was all her fault.

It had been selfish to want Emmy back. If she hadn't given in to loneliness, in to the ache inside for a companion, none of this would have happened.

This was why she must find a way to escape. To fix it. Or at least keep those she loved out of the repercussions her choices started.

Gone were the hopes that she could disappear with Graham. They were more conspicuous together. Somehow, she needed to convince him to find safety with Emmy; then she could lure Flint and his mob away. That was, if she could escape.

The Jeep came to a stop. Jim got out, his footfalls crunching in the snow over to her door. He swung her door open. Her knees trembled as she stepped out, her feet sinking into the snow. Jim tore off her blindfold, ripping away several hairs as he did. She bit her lip to keep from crying out.

Without the blindfold, the sun reflected off the snow and into her eyes. She squinted, the brightness painful. Little by little, a large trailhead sign became clearer.

She rubbed her eyes, trying to bring them back into focus. The letters on the sign aligned. It read

Hinchman's Trail. Beneath the name, it read *Route to Deadman's Bowl*.

Layla sucked in a breath. "This is the trail to Deadman's Bowl?"

Jim grunted as he lifted Emmy's crate onto a sled, along with a few other supplies.

"Are you taking us to Lone Man's Hut?"

He leaned down and tied the crate onto the sled with rope. "Heard of it?"

Yep, she'd heard of it.

It'd been no coincidence that her kidnapper had found her so quickly after the storm. Like someone had anticipated they would take shelter there.

Did Flint use the cabin as a secluded place to do underhanded things? Had she been in his lair when they'd escaped the storm?

It would make sense. The cabin was hardly used—and when it was, never during the day. Skiers only landed there to spend the night before they made a fresh trail down Deadman's Bowl at first light.

Jim pulled his sled to the start of the trail.

Layla's limbs quaked. If he was pulling a sled up the trail, that meant they were traveling the easier route. Right beneath the cornice of snow she and Graham had seen, ready to crumble.

The memory of how it hovered over the trail flashed in front of her mind. Today's sunshine and wind would be loosening that top layer of snow; it would be waiting for only a small trigger to entomb its victim.

"Jim, this isn't a good idea. This area has a high level of avalanche danger."

He pulled the sled's rope around his torso. "Then you had better hush up, hadn't you?"

He jerked his head toward the trail, indicating for her to lead the way.

She glanced around the trees. She could run. She'd come back for Emmy. Somehow. But that's when Jim pulled out a gun and pointed it at Emmy's head.

Layla gasped. "No!"

"Then don't run. It's your choice."

His eyebrow raised with the cock of his gun.

The world shifted beneath Layla's feet, and she almost lost balance. "Okay, please. I won't run."

Layla wanted to punch the smug satisfaction off Jim's face, but he'd won. There would be no escaping this time.

Knowing she was hiking to her demise, her heart like lead, she started up the snowy trail behind Jim.

Her only wish, that she could've told Graham what he meant to her before she died.

TWELVE

Graham had made a terrible mistake.

Beads of sweat saturated his hair beneath his beanie. He clutched his phone in front of him while the wind pelted flakes into his face.

Doubt froze him in place. He needed to do something, but what if he made the wrong choice again? A mistake would lead to death.

Still, he wouldn't find Layla standing there like an ice sculpture. He had to do something. If he found Jim, he'd find Layla. That, he was sure of. Which meant he should start at Jim's. Maybe.

He trudged toward town, his legs heavy like lead. With each step, he became surer of his plan. He forced himself into a jog, then a run, then a sprint, shaking off dread's heaviness.

Once he neared town, he slowed. Staying on the side roads, he skirted the heavily populated areas. He needed to stay as inconspicuous as possible.

Why hadn't he returned to Jim's the moment he'd heard her voice on Ollie's phone? No, instead he had to finish his mission. Even if his gut had shouted for him to return to Layla.

His delay could mean her life.

Why hadn't he anticipated Jim not leaving for work? Jim's spidey senses had probably tingled, and he'd found Layla snooping. He wouldn't have left for work after that.

Had their friendship been a charade all this time? A cover for something underhanded?

Graham thought he might be sick. How could he have swallowed Jim's story about wanting to help him with his investigation? It proved that life really was a do-it-yourself project. He couldn't even trust a friend.

Was there anyone he could trust?

The distance to Jim's stretched longer than Graham remembered. Finally, the peak of the A-frame came into view.

His breath puffed in clouds of mist into the air as he approached, the layers of snow muffling all sounds. His stomach rolled at how quiet it was. Eerie.

Jim's Jeep was gone, tracks streaking from the driveway to the street. Maybe Jim had gone to work. Maybe Layla was safe, inside, unaware of any problem.

But if that was true, what kind of person did that make Layla?

The snow crunched under his boots as he drew closer, keeping to the edge of the trees. He crouched low and crossed the distance to the house. He sank below the kitchen window, listening.

Nothing.

He peeked into the windows, scoping out the house, but everything appeared empty.

He rounded the final corner and stopped.

In the snow beneath a bathroom window was a small pair of footprints as if someone had dropped from the window. Not more than a few feet away, the snow was disheveled, like a struggle had happened.

He scanned the snow until his eyes caught on something lying next to a rock. He bent down for a closer look.

No. His hand gripped the back of his neck. Ollie's phone was shattered. As if someone had thrown it against the rock.

Graham jumped up and ran to Jim's front door, the urgency to find Layla doubling.

The door swung open easily. Unlocked? Since when did Jim leave the door unlocked?

"Layla?" But his voice filled the house with an empty echo.

He circled the rooms again and again, looking for any clues. All he found was an empty dog food bowl and Emmy's fur on the living room rug.

At least Layla had Emmy. He must find them both.

Graham examined the dog bowl. Kibble. Good to know Jim had the decency to feed her.

Wait. He looked closer. A white powder was layered on the bottom of the bowl.

Nausea twisted his gut. He didn't know what the powder was, but he had a good guess.

Jim had drugged Emmy.

Maybe Layla didn't have Emmy—if Emmy was still alive at all.

Graham threw the plastic bowl against the fireplace. It bounced off with a loud bang, and Graham doubled over with his hands on his knees.

Now what?

Sobering thoughts rampaged his mind. Thoughts that said he was too late. That Jim had already delivered Layla to Flint.

He wrapped his hands around his head. No, he wouldn't give up. He had to cling to hope.

If he had to stomp into Flint's office demanding answers, he would. He didn't care if the cops were called on him.

But, most likely, that would backfire. Probably imprisoning him, then how could he help Layla?

He ripped off his beanie and rammed his fingers into his hair.

A memory of something his grandma had said interrupted his spiraling thoughts. Days after his mom had left, she'd said, *You can always rely on God, Graham. He's the one who can make it okay when someone you love lets you down.*

It seemed so long ago. Back then he had brushed the comment off, wallowing in the pain of his own mom not finding him good enough to stay. Instead of turning to God, he'd found comfort in becoming self-reliant.

If he didn't need anyone, then they couldn't let him down.

But now Layla's life hung in the balance. He refused to risk her safety because of his own hang-ups. Because he wanted to do this on his own.

What a hypocrite to insist Layla seek help for her situation when he never wanted to accept help from others. Look where that had led.

Maybe first he needed to start with the One Ollie insisted would never leave him.

"God," he whispered into the empty room. "I can't do this on my own. Please help."

Graham inhaled deeply and closed his eyes. His thoughts cleared, and a calm settled on his heart.

A thought occurred to him. One person may have an idea of where to look for Layla.

Zane.

No, he didn't fully trust Zane, but maybe it was time to take the risk. Zane was the only one who might have a clue about what was happening.

Pulling his beanie down low over his brow, then his hood to keep from being recognized, he raced out the front door. He didn't slow down until he came to Zane's house.

He went to the back door and pounded his fists. He waited a few seconds, then pounded again. No answer.

He raised his fist to pound again but nearly knocked on Zane's forehead when he opened the door.

Graham gasped for breath. "He's taken her."

Zane's back straightened. "What are you talking about? Who's taken who?"

"Layla is gone. I think Jim took her."

Zane's eyes darted behind Graham before he stepped aside to let him in.

He clicked the door shut. "How long ago?"

"I don't know. All I know is, when I went back to Jim's, there were signs of struggle and Ollie's phone was shattered. I think he caught her with Ollie's phone."

Zane dragged a hand down his face. "That isn't good."

"No, it isn't. Now tell me what I should do."

Zane started to pace. "Okay, okay. Let me think."

Graham thought he might burst. "There's no time. We have to find her."

Zane held up his hand. "I know, we just have to be smart."

"Where would he take her? Is there someplace that Flint might own—"

"Lone Man's Hut."

"What? I didn't think anyone owned that place. It's just there for skiers."

"He doesn't own it, the resort does, but it's a secluded place that no one except ski bums know about. I followed him there once when he conducted a secret meeting. I heard them say that Lone Man's Hut was a good place to make people disappear from."

Graham swallowed. "People like Ollie."

"Midday, the area would be deserted. The skiers always take off at first light."

"It's worth a shot."

Zane opened the hall closet, which was filled with ski gear, and pulled out a red backpack. He held it out.

No, not a backpack. An Avalanche Airbag System—an ABS.

"Take this. With the inches over the last few days and today's sun, those layers could be weakening. It's better to be prepared."

Graham took the ABS. It added weight, but the airbag would help keep his body closer to the surface in case of an avalanche. "Thanks."

Zane hesitated. "Look, you shouldn't go alone. I think I should go too."

Maybe he should, but Graham couldn't force himself to agree.

He shook his head. "I've got this. Someone should be around here just in case we're wrong."

Zane studied Graham, then blew out a steady stream of air. "If you're sure, I can check a couple of other places. If I find her, I'll shoot you a cryptic text. We'll meet back here in three hours."

Graham watched as Zane put on his coat without a hint of hesitancy. "Thanks, Zane."

Zane nodded as he rummaged through a bowl sitting on the table next to the front door. He pulled out a set of keys. "Here. Take my Silverado. It's got my snowmobile in the bed."

Zane tossed the keys, and Graham caught them. "I thought I crashed your mobile."

He shrugged. "It needed a new gas line, which

I replaced easily enough. It will get you to that cabin faster."

Graham examined the keys in his hand. Yeah, having someone in his corner felt good. "Thanks."

Zane pointed to a door that looked like it might be the door to the garage. "Go. You're wasting time."

Graham darted through the door to find the Silverado parked in the garage. The truck started right up, and he pulled out onto the street.

Once at the trailhead, he unloaded the snowmobile from the truck and revved up its engine. It was time.

He reached into his coat and flipped on his beacon.

Nothing.

He tried again. Still nothing.

His pulse raced. What choice did he have? He didn't have the time to figure out why his beacon wouldn't turn on.

"Hold on, Layla," he mumbled. "I'm coming."

With a deep breath, he started up the trail.

Without an active beacon.

Layla should be afraid. After all, Jim had led her up a remote trail beneath a cornice of snow that could bury her in an icy tomb. But the fear didn't crack her numbness.

The sound of their boots traipsed through the ice-hardened snow, interrupted only by their gasps from climbing uphill. Hiking was even harder with her hands tied behind her back. Layla's calves burned, but it was insignificant compared to the ache in her heart.

Out here, no one would come looking. No one would know she was missing.

Ollie was gone. Her parents probably still believed whatever Ollie had told them about her disappearance two years ago. Not to mention, she had cut off all ties with friends.

What a failure her life had become. The two years she'd spent hiding, trying to stay alive, would all be for nothing. Just a breath, then she would be gone, and no one would care.

Well, Graham might, a little. At least, he had, before Jim tried to convince him she was lying. Now he probably assumed she'd taken off like his mom.

That part might hurt the most. That Graham now believed her to be just like his mom.

Emmy still lay on her side in the crate, her fur fluttering in the breeze as Jim pulled the sled. Layla could not allow her mistakes to lead to Emmy's demise. Which was why there was no escape. No running to get away. If she played this right, Flint might let Emmy live.

After all, dogs couldn't speak. At least, not in words that could indict a district attorney.

The only way out of her predicament would be if Flint sent her off with a warning. Which would never happen.

Tears wouldn't come. The facts were facts, and there was no use getting emotional over it.

Why had she been so frightened to tell someone? If she had, even if Flint caught her, her story would be in the hands of the authorities and there would be a chance that something good would have come out of it.

Instead, nothing would change.

Her stomach sank.

Maybe it wasn't too late. What if she could leave a message somehow? Or leave something behind that would tell the truth?

But what?

She pictured the small room of the shack. There had to be something in it. Maybe an old camera? Or even a pad of paper she could write a message on? But even if there was, would she be left alone long enough to leave a note?

The trees parted, and she saw the cliff above them, weighted with snow. Her lungs expelled all air.

Wet, fresh snow was too heavy for the weaker layers beneath. She saw what Graham had seen that day. A wall ready to collapse.

Jim quickened up the trail, as if he knew the danger the cliff posed.

She ignored every instinct that clamored for her to turn around. To take cover. But for Emmy, her only option was to follow Jim up the mountainside until they hiked beyond the most dangerous section. Jim shooting Emmy would trigger the avalanche for sure.

Layla held her breath, not daring to breathe. They were so close to safety, yet it was taking too long.

Up ahead sat the cabin, like a prison waiting to confine her. Even if they escaped the avalanche danger, she would only face Flint.

The fear she held at bay enclosed around her, nearly suffocating her.

A sound broke through the whistle of the pines. What was that?

Layla looked behind her shoulder. Something that sounded like a motor came from behind them.

She hesitated even as Jim moved forward.

Could he not hear that?

Her eyes scanned the distance until she spotted it.

A snowmobile moved toward them, launching off a snow berm with reckless abandon.

She squinted to see if she recognized the vehicle. Was it the ski patrol? Or simply someone out for a joyride?

She shoved away the trill of hope that traveled through her. They probably wouldn't get close enough for her to yell for help. Even if they did, she couldn't risk triggering the avalanche.

But the longer she stared, the faster she realized the snowmobile moved with focus and urgency.

And it was coming directly toward them.

Jim appeared beside her with a pair of binoculars. Something low and lethal sounded in his chest.

"Who is it?" She couldn't help the rising pitch of her voice.

It couldn't be Graham. Could it? No, he knew the danger of this trail and would never risk it. Not for her.

The longer she watched, the quicker her heart pounded. The motor rumbled louder as it came closer, the driver going full throttle despite the ledge of snow hovering over the trail.

Jim lowered his binoculars. "Go, go!"

"What is it?"

"Get to the top, now!"

The panic in his voice lit a spark in Layla, and she followed him to the top, clearing the danger zone. Jim dropped the sled's rope and raced to the edge.

Layla stayed next to Emmy. "Who is it?"

He swung his pack in front of him and unzipped it. "It's that boyfriend of yours."

Layla's knees went weak. "Graham?"

He kept digging in his pack for something. "I told him to stay away. I told him you were not who you said you were. Why is he coming?"

Layla didn't answer. Warmth swelled within her, and a smile tugged at the corner of her mouth.

She knew why he was coming. It was because he believed *her*.

Tears blurred the image of the snowmobile coming closer, but rustling pulled her attention away from Graham.

Jim stood at the edge, still rummaging through his pack.

Layla stiffened. "You can't shoot him. He's your friend."

But it wasn't a gun he pulled from his bag. "He was until you came along. Now he's a threat."

His fingers trembled around whatever he clutched in his hand. Something similar in size to a gun, but cylinder shaped.

Layla squinted against the reflection of the sun on the metal. Everything around Layla crashed to a halt as she recognized the two wires attached to the top of the cylinder-like antennae.

A charge.

The wind in the trees sounded like it blew through a tunnel as the blood drained from her head. She ran over to him, slipping in the snow. She scrambled to her feet, but she fell into his arm.

"No, you can't do that! You'll kill him!"

His brow lowered. "Not if he is fast enough."

"Are you crazy? He can't outrace an avalanche."

Jim shoved her away, pushing her backward into a drift. "If it weren't for you, if he hadn't insisted on coming after you, I wouldn't have to."

Before she could get back up, Jim ignited the fuses, waiting until they sizzled before he thrust the charge with impressive strength into the ledge of snow directly above Graham.

"Graham!"

Layla started to run toward the snowmobile, which was now close enough for her to see his reddish hair blowing behind him, but Jim hooked his arm around her waist.

"I want you to watch this," he spat into her ear. "I want you to see what you caused."

"I'm not the one who just threw a two-pound charge to cause an avalanche. This was all you."

"You know nothing. Everything was fine until you came along."

"Graham! Run, Graham!"

But it was too late.

The pop of the charge drowned out her shout as a puff of smoke rose into the air.

As if Graham had sensed the change in the atmosphere, the snowmobile came to a stop.

Then the perfect blanket of snow cracked like glass.

THIRTEEN

Graham must be having another nightmare. A nightmare where Jim, his friend, tossed a charge into a cornice directly above him with the intention of burying him alive.

The blast of the charge echoed around his soul, carrying a resonance of a dream. Clumps of snow traced down the mountain in teardrop patterns.

But it was the eerie calm that awakened him to reality. A hush awaiting a monumental event.

Unable to move, he squeezed the handlebars of the snowmobile. He looked up and saw Jim with his arm looped around Layla's waist.

He seethed with the desire to tear Jim apart, enough so that it scared Graham. Never had he wanted to hurt someone so badly.

He pressed the accelerator, aiming for Jim, but ahead of him, a fracture line sliced down the mountain, blocking his route. The snow between him and where Layla stood rolled faster. Beneath him, the ground shifted, dragging his snowmobile downward.

His muscles tightened as the snow drifted him

farther away from Layla. There was no way to get to her. All he could do was gather his anger and channel it toward surviving. If the avalanche consumed him, he couldn't rescue anyone.

And his best chance—Layla's best chance—was away from the loaded cliff.

A primal growl escaped his throat as he hunched over the handlebars and slammed the accelerator.

Snow sprayed to the side as the snowmobile tipped sideways in his turn. As he straightened the rudders, it teetered before it sped down the mountain. Leaning forward, he weaved between the trees while the rumble increased.

He didn't have to look over his shoulder to see what was behind him. The vibration of the mountainside collapsing shook the handlebars.

In front of him, the snow tumbled faster, becoming ripples. He crouched down farther as if able to speed the snowmobile up with pure will.

The ground in front of him dropped off. Without letting off the accelerator, he aimed for the crag head-on. The snowmobile leaped into the air. He yanked the handlebars back and landed on the back of the rudders.

Momentum carried him faster, but not faster than the snow gathering behind him, its shards pelting him in the back.

He was failing. He couldn't go faster, and his stomach twisted with the realization that the avalanche would swallow him whole.

If he died, who would save Layla? He drew in a

ragged breath. Who would save him? Emmy had been drugged. He didn't have a beacon. How would anyone find him? His chances of survival were slim.

The sound of his heartbeat thrashed in his ears as the approaching wall of snow sounded like a freight train rumbling toward him. The cloud of snow surrounded him, restricting his vision, and the trees became harder to see.

Out of the dimness, a tree materialized in front of him. The nylon of his coat sleeve grazed its trunk as he swerved around it. The action teetered the snowmobile on one blade before it swiveled backward, giving Graham a view of the wall rumbling toward him.

Graham's lungs expelled all air, his muscles frozen.

Who was he to think he could control anything? The grandeur of the power before him diminished any control he'd thought he had.

The snow under his left blade rushed faster than the right, twisting the snowmobile.

With the plume darkening the sun, he lost his sense of direction.

The wave crashed into him. The force jerked the mobile out from beneath him, and he was tossed into the torrent.

His hand trembled as he searched his chest for the release pull for his ABS airbag.

Where was it? His hand patted his chest faster. There. He yanked away the cord, and the bags inflated near his head.

Despite the airbags, he tumbled over and over. Light faded in and out as he was tossed, his body at the mercy of the force of nature. He spun like clothes in a dryer, not knowing which way was up. Didn't know which way was down.

One thought crowded out every other one: *This is it.*

He tried to call out, but snow flew into his mouth, stifling his yell, blocking his breath. Still, his heart cried, "God, save me!"

His outstretched arm smacked around the trunk of a tree, slowing his descent enough to wrap his body around it. He braced his back against a neighboring tree while the one in front shielded him from the full brunt of the snow.

Even so, the snow needled against him, sandblasting the skin of his face. The layers shoved against the tree. It jerked.

The root cracked and its shudder rattled through his body.

With his heart stalled in his chest, the tree rocked before it bent backward into the snow's tide.

To avoid being buried deep with the tree, he let go and somersaulted back into the current. Pressure increased around him, but he resisted it, sporadically waving his arms to stay on top of the layers.

Fatigue trembled in his limbs, and his head told him to give up. To relent to the force that was more powerful than him. But he must stay close to the surface. The closer to the surface, the more likely he'd be found.

But who would come? His arms slowed their frantic paddle.

No one.

He had been so busy being a one-man team that those who might look for him would simply believe his absence was intentional. By the time they decided to look, he would have suffocated.

Exhausted, his arms became limp. The only One who could save him now was God. Would God come through for him? Did God even care enough to help him?

His arms stopped. The momentum of the snow slowed. And everything went dark.

Layla's head spun, threatening to submerge her into unconsciousness.

She wilted in Jim's hold. The force of the crumbling mountainside consumed Graham as if he weighed nothing. A force that also snapped the trees like they were toothpicks.

How could Graham survive such power? A power that reshaped the landscape, taking even boulders in its path.

Layla wanted to hope he could survive, but she couldn't churn anything out of the numbness.

Jim's grip loosened, as if shocked by what he had caused, and, with her hands tied behind her back, she fell forward into the snow. She shoved up to her knees, her eyes fixed on the spot where Graham had disappeared.

He was there, somewhere. She knew it, even if

nothing moved within the calmness settling over the landscape like a reverent awe.

What now? All she had accomplished by fighting for her life was to kill the only man she had ever loved.

How long would it be before someone found their bodies? Would anyone look for her?

Who would look for Graham?

Out of the nothingness within her soul stirred one desperate thought. Someone had to look for him. He had to be found.

And with her being so near the avalanche site, it had to be her. She was his best chance.

If he came for her despite the danger, she would go for him. All she had to do was escape.

Energy trickled back through her body. Lifting her head, she mentally calculated the best route to the debris pile. Her eyes drifted over to Emmy's limp body.

If she ever needed Emmy, it was now. Except she was lying in the crate, motionless.

Father, please wake Emmy up. Graham needs her.

If he was still alive, he had only minutes before he suffocated. After fifteen minutes, his chance of survival cut in half. That is, if he had oxygen at all.

She refocused on the avalanche path. With knees wobbling, she stood. She would need to fight like she had never fought before.

"Don't even think about it," Jim mumbled. He

also stared down the mountain at the debris pile, his face void of emotion.

Layla shook her head. "How can you do this? Stand there and watch as your friend dies?"

Jim stayed silent long enough that Layla didn't think he would answer. Then: "He didn't survive that. No one could."

His voice sounded flat, as if his very soul had been sucked out.

Layla clenched her jaw so tight it hurt. "You don't know that."

He swung his attention to her, a storm brewing within his eyes. "Yes, I do! And you best forget whatever plan you are concocting." He yanked his gun back out of his pocket, his hand trembling. "You could never find him without Emmy."

As if to accentuate his point, he cocked the gun. If he hadn't stopped from killing his friend, killing Emmy would be easy.

Each tick of a second shortened Graham's chances for survival. But if she ran, Emmy would die.

Jim jerked his head toward the cabin. "After you, princess. Flint will be here shortly."

She turned her gaze to Emmy's limp form, then moved toward the cabin, but something made her glance back down at Emmy.

What was that? Did Emmy just twitch? Maybe she'd imagined it. No, Emmy twitched again. Was she waking up?

Layla looked up at Jim, but his focus was on her, oblivious to Emmy showing signs of life.

With hands still tied, she knelt and leaned into the crate's wires. "Come on, Emmy. Graham needs you."

Emmy's eyes fluttered open, then closed again.

"Please, Emmy, wake up."

Emmy stretched out her paws, but when she tried to sit up, she wobbled before she plopped back down.

"Her waking up doesn't change anything, you know. She's still in that crate, and I can shoot her easily enough. Now, get moving. It's cold out here."

Layla hesitated, but Jim gripped her arm and hauled her to her feet. On trembling knees, she walked toward the cabin. After one more look over her shoulder, she stepped through the door.

Time was ticking.

Jim pulled the sled to the door. After untying the crate, he lifted it, Emmy inside. Once in through the doorway, he dropped it to the floor. "My insurance policy stays nearby."

Emmy raised her head and gave a low growl.

Jim slammed on the crate with his palm. "Hush."

Emmy backed up, her backside crashing into the corner of the crate. She jerked forward and shook. Then she started to growl again.

Jim kicked the crate. This time, Emmy hunched low, her growl growing more intense.

With another shake of her head, Emmy appeared more alert. And more agitated. As if confused.

If Layla could get Emmy out of the crate, maybe

together they could escape. Then Emmy could find Graham.

Layla stood to her full height and faced Jim. "You are an evil person."

He narrowed his eyes. "No, this is all your fault. Why did you have to come back at all?"

Layla flinched at the hostility in his tone, but she didn't shrink away. "You aided and abetted killing my brother."

Jim's arms straightened at his side. "I wasn't there—"

"And you just killed Graham."

"I didn't want—"

"And you're about to do the same to me."

"I don't do the dirty work."

Emmy barked. Layla skirted the room until she was closer to Emmy's crate. As she'd hoped, Jim was facing her, matching her movement with a defensive stance. "Causing an avalanche isn't dirty work? You just got rid of a man who thought you were his friend. What's worse, you have no remorse."

"I said that wasn't my fault."

If only Layla could get her hands free of the binding, but every move of her wrists sent pain up her arms. "You threw the charge. No one forced you to."

"Because of you. You ruined everything."

Layla moved into position in front of Emmy's crate. While Jim squared off in front of her, Emmy's bark mixed with snarls.

Jim slapped his hands to his ears. "Get that dog to hush!"

"Why? She knows the truth. She knows you killed both her handlers."

"I said I wasn't there when Ollie died."

"But you allowed it to happen. And now you kidnapped me for the same fate."

Jim's eyebrows lowered into a V as Emmy's snarls grew louder.

Layla raised her chin and lowered her voice to a lethal level. "You have blood on your hands."

In one swift motion, Jim swung his fist, connecting with Layla's cheek. Its force whipped her head to the side, and she stumbled backward, falling against the crate.

Emmy crouched and let out a ferocious bark. Layla blinked hard, trying to see straight, but Jim charged toward her, murder in his eyes, not giving her a chance to recover.

Layla pressed back against the crate, her hands still tied behind her back, until she felt its latch. Her fingers fumbled to grip it as he closed the distance.

There, she grasped it. She released the latch and swung the door opened.

Emmy leaped out with a snarl. She jumped onto Jim, knocking him down as the gun in his hand collided with the floor.

Jim lunged toward the gun, but Emmy blocked him, hunched low. Trapped on the ground, he backed away. Emmy's low growl held him hostage.

Stickiness spread over Layla's hand. She twisted

to see over her shoulder to her hand. Blood dripped from a fresh gash.

What had happened to her hand? She hadn't noticed the pain, but blood gushed from the wound.

She scanned the crate. In the lower right hand, a sharp edge of metal had broken away from the crate. Maybe sharp enough to cut away a plastic strip cutting off the circulation in her wrists.

Holding her breath, she raised the strap, cinching her wrists to the edge, and sliced. She slipped, cutting her wrist again. Gritting her teeth, she tried once more.

Jim inched backward toward the gun, Emmy following him with her teeth exposed.

Layla couldn't let Jim get to that gun. She pressed the strap harder against the pointed edge.

It snapped.

Jim reached the gun and clutched it in his hand. He stood slowly, pointing it at Emmy.

Without rubbing the wounds the plastic left behind, Layla launched to her feet and grabbed the shovel lying on the floor, the same one Graham had used to defend her earlier.

Jim cocked the gun. "I've always hated dogs."

With a yell, Layla swung the shovel into his head.

Jim staggered forward, the gun slipping from his hand before he slumped to the floor.

Emmy watched Jim fall, licking her jowls. Then, with a whimper, she crossed over to Layla and pressed into her legs.

Breathless, Layla framed Emmy's face between her hands. "It's okay, girl. I'm okay. But we have to go."

She opened the door and started to head out but stopped short. She backtracked and picked up the gun.

With trembling hands, she shoved it into her pocket. No, she didn't know how to use it, but she couldn't leave it for Jim to find. "Come on, Emmy. Let's go save Graham."

Layla returned to the top of the avalanche's path. Nothing below moved, except the newly exposed snow blowing into ripples made by the wind.

She needed a quick way down to the debris pile. Every minute counted, and she had already wasted several trying to get away from Jim.

With Emmy at her heels, she ran back into the cabin, searching for a set of skis or something she could use. At first glance, she saw nothing, but as she ran back outside, she stopped, Emmy slamming into the back of her knees.

The sled that Jim had used to pull Emmy up the trail would work.

She ran back inside the cabin and grabbed the shovel smudged with Jim's blood. Grabbing the sled's rope, she pulled it to the top of the slope and aimed it down. She sat on it before she coaxed Emmy to sit between her legs. With one scoop of the shovel, she pushed the sled off the crest of the hill.

Snow sprayed into her flushed face as Emmy

looked straight ahead, probably already focused on her job.

As they slid lower, trees and debris stuck up out of the snow. Layla maneuvered the sled around most of the debris until a large root launched the sled into the air.

Emmy bailed out, then raced to meet Layla as she tumbled into the snow.

Layla's body rolled until a bank of snow stopped her descent.

Emmy licked her face. "I'm okay, girl."

But when she stood, her leg buckled underneath her. No, she couldn't be hurt. She had to press through the pain. Graham was depending on her.

She forced herself to stand again, ignoring the fire burning in her knee, and stumbled down the remaining few feet.

Emmy stayed next to her side, her ears perked and fully alert.

They arrived near the spot she'd seen Graham engulfed by the avalanche. She stopped, scanning for any signs of him.

Emmy whimpered, her body taut as she waited for the cue.

Layla leaned down until the softness of Emmy's ear brushed her cheek. With the authority Ollie had taught her to use, she pointed and said, "Emmy, go find."

FOURTEEN

Nothing was as cold as a tomb of snow.

A tomb getting colder, draining away the warmth of his body.

It didn't feel much different from his nightmares, only the tremor coursing up his spine didn't come from the ice molding his limbs into place. Nor from his struggle to inhale. Nor from the penetrating chill.

No, instead, it came from knowing he had failed Layla. She was at Jim's mercy, and he couldn't do anything to stop it.

The cold seeped deeper through his coat. The chills had started in his feet, which were now numb, and traveled up his legs. The sound of his teeth chattering echoed around the small air pocket.

He twisted within his cocoon, trying to loosen the snow's grip, but the only thing he gained was a piercing pain up his leg.

A groan escaped his lips. Without seeing his body, he knew his leg was twisted at an unnatural angle.

But it didn't matter how much pain he was in. All

that mattered was Layla. She may be experiencing something more agonizing than any contorted limb.

He squeezed his eyes closed against the terrible images. Against the worst his imagination could conjure.

His breath came in gasps. The air pocket he had created immediately after being buried with his own breath and spit had only gained him a few extra minutes. If he didn't get his breathing under control, the gasping would zap his oxygen.

How had he ended up here? How had everything spun out of control so fast?

Jim.

All this happened because he'd missed the signals that Jim was working with Flint. Conversations and interactions rolled through his mind, but not one pointed to Jim's capability for murder. And not just a random murder, but the murder of someone who had called him friend.

What clue had he missed? Or was Graham so wrapped up in fixing problems that he'd missed the warning signs?

Mr. Do It Himself. Look where his manifesto had gotten him.

What would have happened if he had accepted Zane's offer to come with him? Maybe Zane would be there to dig him out so they could help Layla together. Unless he ended up buried beside Graham.

Still, there must have been something he could have done differently to not end up here.

His gasps became shorter.

Come on, Graham. Take charge of your body. Slow it down.

But he couldn't. He didn't have control of anything.

How dense could he be? It took an avalanche to figure out he never did have control.

There was only One who could control the forces of nature. Only One whom he could depend on.

Something came to mind that he could've done differently. He could've prayed. He could've asked the One who did have control about what to do next instead of fumbling with what he thought might work.

If he had done that from the start, released control to God, maybe he wouldn't be buried. Maybe Layla wouldn't be fighting for her life in a raunchy ski shack.

But it was too late to undo the mess he'd created. All he could do now was pray for God to intervene. No, not intervene for him. It might be too late for him. But for Layla. She was the only one who mattered.

"God," his raspy voice echoed off the icy chamber. He forced his lungs to take in a sip of air. "I relent. It isn't up to me to fix everything. Please help Layla."

He blew out a trembling breath, and his body went limp. He had released Layla back into the hands of the One who really could rescue her.

Time became irrelevant as oxygen drained away

from his shuddering muscles. Pressure increased in his throbbing head as he demanded his lungs take another breath.

Things became darker.

Graham was transported to the top of a mountain. His skis teetered over a ledge of fresh snow. He held his breath, awestruck by the blanket of undisturbed white.

Unbroken powder, waiting. Beckoning.

He tipped from the crevice to fall down the mountain. Gravity settled down on his body as his skis sank into the powder, answering a deep-seated craving. Pure, awesome. Fantastic. Not unlike what a kiss from Layla might be.

Layla.

He could almost hear her calling his name.

He opened his eyes. A ringing in his ears grew louder and louder, until the magic drained away to a world of darkness. He gasped, fighting for air.

"Graham!"

There it was again, her voice. It sounded so clear he could have assumed she stood right above him. But it couldn't be her. She was trapped. Kidnapped.

Sleep. He needed sleep. He just felt so tired.

Wait. What was that sound?

It sounded liked paws. Emmy?

No, hallucinations must be kicking in. Poor Emmy had been drugged. He didn't even know to what extent. She could have been killed by whatever powder had coated that dish.

So why did he hear a whine, followed by a string of barks?

He knew that bark. Had seen Emmy scratch at the snow while using that same bark. It was her "I found something" bark in the training field.

The scratching grew louder.

Then he heard Layla's voice. "Graham? Graham? Are you there?"

He tried to answer, but he couldn't muster the energy. It couldn't be real, anyway. How would she get away?

He refused to believe it. Yet, he felt paws pull at his hair as they dug.

He moaned. Weak and barely there, but if he wasn't dreaming, he had to let them know to keep digging.

"That's him, Emmy." He heard a sob break loose as something else dug around him. "Keep digging, Emmy. He's there."

The snow over his head broke free, releasing the warmth of sunlight onto his forehead. Then the snow from around his face was shoved away, and he inhaled the sweetest breath he had ever taken.

Tears didn't come—they were probably frozen—but he wanted to cry. If only to make sure he wasn't dreaming.

Cold hands wrapped around his cheeks. "Graham, you're alive. Oh, thank You, God. You are alive."

Emmy gave him a slobbery kiss on his cheek.

He couldn't respond. All he could do was breathe in the crisp oxygen that tickled his lungs.

"I'm going to get you out of here, Graham. You're going to be okay. Where are you hurt? Does your back hurt? Your neck?"

His leg hurt—or at least, it used to before the numbness had set in—but he couldn't form the words.

She smoothed her hands around him, scooping more snow away from his face. "It's okay. Don't speak. I'll get you out of there."

He heard a shovel bang against the snow. Again and again, the scoop dug into the top layers of snow, but he could hear she wasn't making much progress. The snow had hardened, and his body was too deep.

Yet she kept trying until he heard the crack of the shovel's shaft.

"No, no, no," she mumbled. She fell to her knees and dug the broken scoop into the snow.

Graham's eyes slid closed. "It was probably an old shovel, anyway. Who knows how long it sat inside the hut."

She leaned down and kissed his forehead, pushing the hair away from his face. "I will find a way to get you out."

His teeth began to chatter harder, as if to warn them time was running out.

Emmy must have noticed, because she circled around him before lying down next to his head, emitting as much warmth as she could.

The lines in Layla's forehead deepened. He saw the urgency in her eyes.

The snow was lowering his core temperature fast.

If he didn't get out and warm up soon, it just might be too late.

The expanse of wilderness echoed around Layla's heart.

Nobody. There was nobody to help her. And she was running out of time.

She wandered a few more feet away and cupped her hands around her mouth. "Hello!"

The white landscape's insulation swallowed her voice. No one outside of ten feet could hear her.

Still, she tried again. "I need help! Anyone, please help!"

A gust of wind picked up the snow around her into a mini torrent, as if to blow her attempt away.

She tried to stir up energy for another shout, but it fizzled into a weak "Please, anyone."

Was God even there? Would He help if she could muster enough faith to pray again?

She had started off her journey into hiding by praying every day, but as day after day turned into months, then years, hopelessness had dissolved her prayers.

But now, with Graham's life hanging in the balance, it was her only lifeline. The only thing she had left.

"Please, God..." she sniffed and wiped her running nose with her sleeve. "Send help."

She waited. She didn't really expect an immediate answer, or maybe she did, but the silence weighed heaviness onto her heart.

They needed a rescue, not silence.

Her muscles became limp. Her knees nearly gave way as she turned back toward Graham.

Emmy continued to hover near Graham. Even when Layla had wandered away a distance to call for help, Emmy had stayed next to him.

She approached Graham, but he didn't move, didn't acknowledge her, ice encrusting his hair.

Alarm sparked, reenergizing her limbs. She ran toward him. *Oh, please, God, don't let him be dead.*

"Graham!"

Only a few yards away, her foot caught on a clump of snow, sending her forward to her knees. She slid the remaining distance on her belly.

His eyes opened. The corner of his mouth twitched with a smile that failed. "Hey there, beautiful. I wondered if you left me for someone better looking."

Her lungs reopened, allowing her to inhale sharply, but she didn't have time to bask in relief. With gloved hands, she began to shovel the snow away from his neck. "Enough with the jokes. I have to get you out of here."

Graham's eyes slid closed as he inhaled a deep breath. "So I guess that means that no one is coming."

"All you need is me."

He chuckled, but it ended with a croupy cough. "Sweetheart, you are the strongest woman I've ever met, but it's going to take more than your bare hands to get me out of here."

She paused her shoveling. He was right. She knew he was, but what other choice did she have? Go and get a different shovel from the cabin? The same cabin where her attacker may be waking up inside?

No, it would take too long to hike back up. Besides, she couldn't leave Graham.

She continued digging. "I'm not giving up until you're out of there."

Graham coughed again. "No one's coming."

She heard it in his voice—hopelessness. Like he was ready to give up. She stopped digging long enough to point her finger into his face. "Don't."

"Don't what?"

"Just—don't. Don't stop trying."

"There is nothing that we can do, Layla. No one is coming. I knew no one would come."

Her hands slowed down as her shoulders rounded. "This is all my fault."

"No. Don't go there. Let's not talk about who is at fault."

She sped up her digging, but she had only achieved a few inches. Emmy joined her on the other side. Like she sensed the urgency.

"Layla, stop, please. Just sit and talk to me. You can't talk to me if you are trying so hard."

Layla shook her head. "No."

"Layla, look at me."

She kept digging.

"Please."

She stopped but didn't remove her hands from the hole she was making slow progress in. She raised her eyes to his, following his instruction, but she wished she hadn't because the tears she held at bay began to fill her eyes.

"Don't give up, Graham."

"Layla, I need you to know that…that I l—"

A cough racked his body, and she smoothed his hair away from his face.

Layla swallowed against the growing lump in her throat. "Shh…don't try to speak. Conserve your energy."

He shook his head. "No." His voice trembled, as if he had to muster his remaining strength. "I want to tell you—"

Emmy bolted to attention, her body rigid at full attention.

Layla sniffed. "What is it, girl?"

Emmy didn't glance at Layla. Instead, the fur on her back steepled, and she stepped forward.

Scanning the trees downhill, Layla stood, her body stiff. Something was coming.

Then she heard the voice in the distance. "Graham!"

Layla sucked in a breath. Hopelessness wouldn't make her imagine voices, would it?

"Graham!"

No, she was sure she heard someone that time.

Emmy's tail started to wag, and she inched forward.

The brush next to the tree line rustled before a golden retriever in a red vest broke through. The dog charged toward them, barking. Emmy ran toward the dog, then ran back to Graham, also barking.

Layla blinked hard when she saw not just one man, but an entire crew emerge from the forest with poles and shovels in their hands. Another dog, a yellow lab, rounded the crew and sprinted toward them.

That was when she recognized Zane leading the crew.

Layla raised her arms above her head and waved. "Zane!"

As the crew raced closer, Layla fell to her knees. "They're here, Graham. Your ski team, they're here."

Graham's eyes closed. He probably thought he was hallucinating.

Zane stopped in front of them, huffing. "Do you always have to be a troublemaker, Graham?"

Graham didn't laugh. "Yet you came, anyway."

Zane motioned for the crew to get to work. "It's what I do."

The crew began to dig with shovels, chipping away at the hardened snow.

Zane leaned down and took Graham's pulse at his neck. His brow pinched tight. "When I heard the

avalanche warning go off out here, I knew somehow you were in trouble."

"Then get me outta here."

Zane blew out a sigh. "Even when buried by an
avalanche, you have to be so pushy."

Once they'd cleared the snow away from Graham's body, they examined his neck and back.
Then they splinted his leg before they pulled him
out from the snow and onto a toboggan, where Zane
continued to check all vitals.

They worked together with precision and knowl-
edge, each person fulfilling their part. A team.

Emmy inched toward Graham, as if worried she
might carelessly hurt him, and nudged him with
her nose. Graham reached up with a shaking arm
and scratched her ears.

Emmy pressed her head into Graham's hand,
then lifted her paw and looped it over his arm.

Graham paused. An emotion Layla couldn't quite
describe crested his face, but her heart swelled. The
corner of his mouth pulled up into a weak smile.

He nodded as he began to scratch again. "Good
girl, Emmy. Good girl."

The crew wrapped thermal blankets around him,
but they didn't look warm enough to keep him from
shivering. She winced when he groaned.

Before the crew set off down the mountain, Graham's eyes found hers. He gave a small smile, but
it did nothing to convince her that he was okay.
Nothing about this was okay.

Layla stuffed her hands under her arms as a tear trickled down her face.

As one of the crew members began to pull the toboggan down the mountain, Emmy followed a few steps before stopping. She gave a little whimper before she backtracked to Layla's side and sat down, her eyes watching the descending crew.

Layla ran her hand down Emmy's back. "This is wrong, Emmy. He should have never been in that avalanche in the first place."

From her gut, she began to seethe. How dare Jim do this to Graham? How dare Flint steal two years of her life, wanting her to live afraid?

She was done. She was done running scared just like Flint wanted.

He wanted her running. Wanted her so scared she never uttered a word about what she saw.

For two years, he had been winning.

No more.

"He's pretty cold, showing the early signs of hypothermia." Layla startled. She hadn't even noticed Zane approach. "But I think—or at least, I hope—we got to him on time. I'm sure his leg is broken, but he isn't nearly as banged up as he could've been. It really is a miracle."

The muscle in her jaw throbbed. She'd forgotten that Jim had hit her. She gently probed what was sure to be a bruise as she watched the team drag Graham down the slope.

Zane inhaled. "Bailey said she could take Emmy for a few days while you recover."

Layla nodded, but that wasn't what she wanted to talk about right now. "What do you know? About Flint?"

He ignored her question and put his arm around her shoulders. "Come on, let's get you checked out too. Then we'll talk."

Layla jerked out of his grasp, stumbling backward. "No, tell me. What do you know about Flint?"

Zane scratched his cheek with his gloved knuckle.

She narrowed her eyes. "This needs to be over."

He held her gaze. "First, I need you to tell me about why you ran off two years ago."

Layla didn't hesitate. Only jerked a nod. "Okay. Fine."

"I mean everything. I need you to trust me before I can trust you."

Layla nodded again. She was done hiding.

It was time to fight.

FIFTEEN

"I'll do whatever it takes to see these men behind bars. Even if I have to confront Flint myself."

The words filtered into Graham's unconscious mind, startling him awake. The bland ceiling tiles above him swam with a rainbow of colors. Where was he, again?

He squeezed his eyes closed. When he reopened them, the tiles came into focus, as did the throbbing pressure pulsing down his leg, which was locked into place.

The fingers of the hand that didn't hurt probed the other arm. Soft gauze ran around his wrist.

That's right. In one slideshow after another, he remembered being life-flighted to a hospital in Denver. Not his first helicopter ride, but his first as a patient, where every bump and tilt made him grit his teeth in pain.

Everything after that became fuzzy.

Now, as he knew it would, Layla's voice beckoned him back to reality.

So why did the words not match what he knew about her? Was he still dreaming?

"It's risky," a man's voice said. "Maybe too risky, but it might work." It sounded like Zane. Why had he stuck around?

"It has to work."

They sounded like they were somewhere off in the distance. Maybe in the hallway?

"I think I might have a plan," Zane said, "but a lot can go wrong. We need to make sure everything is well thought out."

"Fine. This needs to be over, one way or another."

The venom in Layla's voice made him flinch. That didn't sound like his sweet Layla. The Layla who had only wanted to hide.

Zane released a slow sigh. "But jumping in without taking the time to weigh all the angles is careless. I've been in Silver Ridge too long to allow recklessness to spoil everything."

"This doesn't have to include you. They won't even know you're involved in the planning. It's just me. The only one at risk is me."

Zane didn't respond immediately. He was probably thinking the same thing Graham was—that she needed some sense talked into her. Where did this rashness emerge from? The last he knew, Layla's whole mission was to evade trouble, not run into it with guns blazing.

Finally, Zane said, "Even so, I'm not going to send you in on a suicide mission. It accomplishes nothing."

Thank you, Zane. Speak that truth.

Layla huffed. "I've already sacrificed two years of my life because I've been afraid. I'm not going to let fear stop me anymore."

"There's a thin line between courage and recklessness, Layla."

"I don't care. I'm marching into Flint's office and demanding answers."

"Over my dead body." Graham didn't care that he'd be caught eavesdropping. He wasn't about to let Layla destroy herself.

The hallway became silent before Layla meandered into the room wearing a rosy disposition that didn't fool anyone. "Hey there. Glad to see you back to the land of the living."

Way too cheerful after what he'd just heard. "You aren't going anywhere near Flint."

Zane stepped in behind her. "You had us a little nervous. You've been in and out these past couple of days. How're you feeling?"

Couple of days? Had he been here that long?

It didn't matter. He blinked hard to refocus.

"Whatever plan you've concocted isn't going to happen, so you may as well forget it."

The fake smile didn't even droop from her face. And was that a bruise on her jaw? The sharp point of anger jabbed at his gut.

She reached for his good hand and squeezed it. "There is nothing you need to worry about. I'm just so thankful to see your eyes open."

Graham's body stiffened. "No, stop! Drop the act, would you?"

Zane began to back out of the room. "I think I'll go find some coffee. Be back in a while."

Finally, the fakeness was wiped from her face, replaced by a raw desperation. Or maybe pure brokenness. Whatever it was, it manifested into a lethal look in her eyes. "I saw you buried. I thought you were dead. It is an image that replays constantly in my head. I'm not going let Jim get away with that."

The edge in her voice turned Graham cold. He squeezed her fingers. "But I didn't die. See? I'll be okay. I survived. You survived. Let's keep it that way."

"For how long, Graham? How long before they come after us again?"

Graham hadn't been awake long enough to ponder that question. Now it settled over him, a wet blanket of reality.

Yet all that mattered was them. They had survived, and he wasn't about to throw it away on some vigilante mission.

He gazed into her eyes without blinking. "Then we run."

She closed her eyes and shook her head. "No. Not anymore. I've wasted two years of my life—"

"But now we can do it together. You and me. And Emmy."

She scanned the ceiling, biting her lip.

"You won't have to be alone any longer. We'll be a family. A fresh start, just you and me."

At the word *family*, she inhaled sharply. A cleansing breath that he only hoped was her common sense returning.

"Layla, home is wherever we are together. I'll go wherever you want to go."

She started to shake her head again.

Graham rushed on before she offered a rebuttal. "Even Arizona, where there is no snow. Flint won't think of looking for a ski bum in Arizona."

The corner of her mouth twitched. "Graham, I—I—"

"Please say yes," he whispered.

Layla stilled. He watched as tears flooded into her eyes. She breathed out his name: "Graham."

He looked at her fingers entwined within his. A perfect fit. Like they'd belonged together from the very beginning. "It's not an empty gesture, Layla. My heart started beating again when you walked into my life. It took a near-death experience for me to realize I don't want to waste any more time. Please, let's start fresh."

Layla licked her lips. "I think that maybe you are on some pain meds, and—"

Graham pulled her down tenderly until she relented to lower her lips to his. Her kiss felt full of emotion mixed with hesitancy. Then he felt her tears on his lips, and they soured in his mouth.

He loosened his grip on her arm, and she straightened, her eyes rimmed with red. "What's the matter, Layla? It'll be okay. We'll get lost in the crowd and—"

"And always be hiding. Don't you see? We'd be

staying one step ahead of destruction year after year."

Graham's mind went blank. She was saying no.

"I want to be with you, Graham. Maybe go on an actual date. But I'm tired of hiding. We have to finish this first."

"Not at the risk of your life, we don't."

"What kind of life would we have always running? Always looking behind our back? You've said that yourself."

"Yeah, before I knew how deep the corruption went. Look what happened with Jim. Didn't he give you that bruise on your jaw?"

Her hand flew to hide her bruise. "Which is why we have to finish this."

Graham stared at her. He couldn't believe this was the same Layla who'd made him promise to never tell a soul about what she'd seen. "It's not worth your life, Layla."

She sniffed. "A wise man once told me that a life on the run is no life at all."

Graham stiffened. It wasn't fair, fighting him with his own words.

He leaned his head back, suddenly very tired. "So, you're willing to sacrifice what we can become to fight a battle you can't win?"

"No, that's not what I'm saying at all."

"Then what are you saying? Because I already lost Ollie. I cannot—I refuse to lose you too."

Layla's jaw slackened. "Life and death don't rest in your hands, Graham."

"Maybe not, but that doesn't mean I will allow you to go on a suicide mission."

Layla straightened, her face taking on a shade of red. "You know what, I played it safe. I tried to pretend I could stay ahead of Flint one step at a time, but you know what I discovered?"

"What?"

"This isn't just about me. There is something going on bigger than either of us. What kind of person am I if I ignore the other innocent people who could get hurt from my inaction?"

Exhaustion weighed heavy on Graham. He knew the answer. Cowards. But he couldn't admit that to her. Instead, he could only answer with the word he feared the most: "Dead."

Her shoulders rounded forward. "If I can't stop him with my testimony, then who can?"

Graham searched her eyes. "Before I met you, I believed life was a do-it-yourself project. For the first time since my mom dropped me like something hot, I want to trust again. To believe that I could have someone on my side. I'm willing to take a chance, to believe, that you and I can be a team in life."

"We can, Graham."

Graham's head was heavy as lead as he shook it from side to side. "No, because trust requires sacrificing one's own agenda."

"Agenda? Really? So, everything is good between us unless I go against your wishes. Is that how it is? This isn't an agenda, Graham. This is what I truly believe God wants me to do. He's giving me the courage to do it. I need you to trust me."

"But I don't."

The words slipped out before he could stop them. He didn't really mean it, but it was too late. All color drained from Layla's face as his own shock rippled over his heart.

The apology lingered on his tongue, but he couldn't say it. Even if he loved her, his love would never be enough.

Layla's breath trembled. "Graham, this is something I have to do."

She hesitated, her eyes averted, then walked out of the hospital room.

Graham almost called after her, but those words caught in his throat.

He closed his eyes, the pain in his heart sharper than the pain in his leg.

"You're an idiot."

The words brought Graham's attention to Zane, who stood in the doorway with his arms crossed.

Great. Zane's lecture posture. Did he really deserve this while lying in a hospital bed? Not to mention, the guy had no cup of coffee. Which meant he'd been eavesdropping.

"Save it, Zane. This has nothing to do with you."

"Nope, it doesn't. But you are an idiot."

Graham rolled his eyes.

Zane pointed at Graham. "You know what that

girl has been through. Don't you realize that her testimony could put Flint in jail for a long time?"

"If they believe her."

Zane gave an ironic laugh. "That's low. Not so long ago, you believed her, didn't you?"

Graham couldn't look him in the eye any longer. Not without guilt gnawing at his stomach.

Zane rubbed his hand down his face. "Look, I think I have a plan that could possibly dethrone the prince of the DA's office. A real plan. I wasn't going to let her be reckless, Graham."

Graham shrugged, but his insides were tearing to shreds. Was he being selfish? Maybe a little, but this had nothing to do with him trying to control her. Even if he was, it was only because he wanted her safe.

"If you search deep within yourself, Graham, you don't want to run from this. If you and Layla ever want to marry, you'll want to with her family present. In broad daylight. If this plan works, she could go home. You two can live normal lives. Isn't that worth the risk? Think about her happiness."

"I'd rather be with Layla on the run than have her be dead." Or in jail.

But an unwelcome thought warred within his head. Would she truly be happy when he knew her greatest desire was to put down roots? To find a home?

No. She wouldn't.

Zane released a slow breath. "Think about it, Graham. If you want to help, I'll be pulling together a team to hammer out the plan, and I want you to be a part of it. Choose not to be an idiot."

Then Zane left, leaving Graham alone with his thoughts.

Darkness settled on the streets of Silver Ridge as Layla made her way to Zane's house. With her hair tucked in her maroon beanie and red plastic rim glasses, she remained in the shadows.

A week later and Layla's frustration had only grown. After everything they'd been through, how could Graham not see the importance of stopping Flint once and for all?

If Graham expected her to follow him to Phoenix like a puppy, he had another thing coming.

These past few days, she'd stayed in Denver, hiding in a cheap motel she paid for with a credit card under a pseudonym provided by Zane. She'd returned moments ago, and she'd do well to remember that even the cops were looking for her here.

Having Emmy remain with Zane's sister helped her hide, but she missed her dog.

She hadn't seen Graham since their conversation. Didn't even know when he'd be released.

Not once had he tried to contact her. That part probably made her the angriest. Or hurt. She didn't quite know.

But if she stopped being angry, the pain might catch up to her and fold her in its grasp.

No, it was better to growl in frustration than succumb to the loneliness on her heels.

She unzipped her black coat and allowed the evening's arctic temperatures to cool her down.

If she had to expose Flint without Graham, fine. If the plan went south and their last words were ones of anger, fine.

Her chest constricted tight. No, not fine. Not fine at all.

She stiffened her lips. It didn't matter. All this turmoil, all this pain disguised as anger fueled her purpose. To bring Flint down.

Layla approached Zane's front door; the porch lights were off. The only hint that she was in the right place was the light filtering through the curtains of his front window.

She pulled back her shoulders, then rapped her knuckles against the door.

The door opened. Layla didn't smile as she nodded to greet Zane. He scanned the street behind her before he stepped aside to let her in.

Layla started to enter, but a ball of black fur nuzzled into her legs.

She leaned down and rubbed Emmy's ears. "Oh, Emmy, I've missed you."

Layla paused. Inside, an audience of three others watched.

She straightened, clearing her throat. Would she have to tell all these people her story?

Nothing like being the awkward party guest who didn't know anyone.

A tight smile lifted the corner of her lips as she stepped inside and closed the door.

The watchful gazes of those in the room made her itch. She folded her arms around her middle. She could do this. These people were on her team. No reason to be nervous.

Still, she had to force herself not to yank away the bottled water Zane offered and guzzle it.

Emmy wandered over to lie beside a golden retriever at the feet of a woman sitting on the couch. The dogs appeared to know each other, but Layla didn't recognize her.

Zane pointed toward the woman. "Layla, this is Bailey, my sister. And her avy dog, Banner."

Bailey had the same dark features as Zane but without the severe clench of his jaw. Layla returned her smile, even if it shook a little.

Zane moved to stand behind the other woman in a wooden rocking chair. She wore black slacks and a red silk shirt with a long silver necklace. Her black suit jacket hung on the back of the chair.

"This is Nora. She's a paralegal in Flint's office."

Which explained the business attire. Layla smoothed her hand along her sweatshirt. Maybe she should have at least worn her hair down instead of in a messy bun.

Zane fist-bumped the other man, who had frosted tips styling his hair. "And this is Coby, a friend and coworker who I trust. We served together in the army."

She nodded at his suave "Hey."

"Guys, this is Layla. The one I told you about. Tell them what you told me."

A tremble began to course through Layla's arms. She hugged the bottle of water tighter to her body. Each set of eyes waited for her to speak.

Layla swallowed. After hiding her story for so long, the words wouldn't form. She'd expected to feel vulnerable tonight as they finalized the plan to catch Flint once and for all. She'd promised herself she wouldn't clam up. But she hadn't known there would a crowd.

And not one of them was Graham.

She hadn't realized the courage he'd given her before. Oh, how she wished he was there. Even just to stand next to her while she spoke.

She shuddered. No more *what if*s. It was time to be brave.

"I, well, I saw Flint kill a man." Did her voice sound as mouselike as it felt? She cleared her throat. "He's chased me for the last two years. Nearly killed me a few days ago with the help of his accomplice."

She waited for the arguments, the opposition to her accusations, but no one even raised an eyebrow. Not one person seemed shocked from the revelation. Instead, the group passed around a secret look that Layla didn't understand.

After a beat of silence, Zane motioned to the others. "Two years ago, our friend Ryan Murphey disappeared. He was working for Flint as a CPA, when he mumbled to me once, 'Flint's books don't add up. I don't have a good feeling about it.' A week later, we were told that he went on a backpacking trip to Alaska and then fell off a cliff."

Layla sucked in a breath. "Kind of like how my brother accidentally fell off a cliff."

Zane paused and looked her in the eye. "Exactly. Sometimes Ryan would go on excursions, but he never left without telling one of us. We believe Flint killed him, and we made a pact to uncover the truth."

Two years ago? Was it just a coincidence or could it possibly be related to the night she saw Flint commit murder?

Coby leaned forward with his elbows on his knees, concern lowering in his brow. "You should tell the authorities. A testimony like this would be powerful."

Layla stifled her scoff. "He's already tried to frame me as an intruder who broke into his office. The cops want to bring me in. Who do you think they'll believe? Some girl who shows up after being away for two years or the district attorney?"

Coby's face conceded her point.

"So, what's the plan?" Nora asked.

Layla picked at the label on her water bottle. "I want to confront Flint and secretly record his confession to the murder."

Coby slid a hand down his face.

Bailey sighed. "Don't you think that plan has a lot of holes in it?"

"Look, everyone—" Zane's voice took charge "—I have an idea, but I need your help. First, Nora,

I need you to clear Flint's schedule tomorrow and secure a nearby room in his building."

Nora's eyebrows raised, but she followed up with a nod.

"Then Coby and Bailey, I need you to run interference in case anyone tries to come into the building. Have Banner play dead or something. Play the sympathy card. That always seems to work."

Coby and Bailey shot each other a glance before they also nodded.

Zane blew out a long breath before he turned toward Layla. "Layla, are you sure about this?"

No. Not one bit. "Yes. He buried Graham in an avalanche. If I don't do something, someone else is going to get hurt."

At least, that was the mantra repeating over and over in her head.

Zane stared at her, his eyes penetrating to the truth. Without removing his gaze, he nodded. "Can you find a way to keep him talking?"

Layla's tongue turned to sandpaper. "Yes. I think I know how."

"Thinking can ruin this—"

"Yes. I can do it."

His eyes narrowed as if he wanted to read her mind. He opened his mouth, but Emmy bolted to her feet, her body on full alert. Banner followed Emmy's lead.

Everyone in the room held their breath. No one moved, as if a twitch might snap the tension in the room.

Then Layla heard it—the shuffling of footsteps coming up the porch steps. They sounded labored. A step, then a slide, as if whoever it was had to drag one foot.

Had they just been discovered?

The group looked to Zane for his cue. Run or stand?

The doorknob jiggled. Zane motioned for everyone to get down as he pulled a gun out from his concealed holster. Without a sound, he approached the door.

Layla's heart slammed in her chest, and she struggled to inhale. She curled tightly between the chair and the wall. Emmy stood rigid in the open living room floor.

With one last glance around the room to make sure everyone had found cover, Zane opened the door in a fluid motion and aimed his gun directly into the chest of the intruder.

The man's hands raised above his head, his crutches leaning again his body. "It's me."

Layla's body went limp at Graham's voice.

He was here. Her heart skipped a beat. Her muscles relaxed, and she started to move toward him, but then froze. Why was he here? Was he here to stop her?

Well, he wouldn't. Why couldn't he understand that?

Zane lowered his gun. "You couldn't have called first so I knew you were coming?"

Graham didn't answer. Instead, his gaze roamed

the room. Her breath rushed out when it locked with hers. She saw the turmoil within him. Turmoil that echoed her own.

His jaw shifted, obviously not caring that the chill from the open door frosted the room.

His throat bobbed as he swallowed. "Sorry I'm late."

SIXTEEN

Graham hated to admit it, but Zane was right: he really was an idiot. Especially now, standing with the help of his crutches in Zane's doorway, rendered mute by Layla's gaze.

An ache to explain himself swelled, yet he couldn't form words. What was wrong with him? Was it so hard to ask for forgiveness?

He thumped his fingers one at a time against the handle of his crutch. She didn't look happy to see him. Maybe a little surprised, but not happy. Strike number one.

"Glad you could join us, Graham," Zane said.

Us? He forced his gaze away from Layla and found three other people in the room, all of whom watched with unblinking stares.

He fumbled into the room and swung the door closed with his crutch. "Sorry. I didn't mean to interrupt."

Zane holstered his weapon and nodded toward a vacant chair, which Graham plunked down in. "I didn't think you were going to make it."

The pulse in Graham's leg told him he might be pushing it by coming. "Yeah, well, neither did I."

Layla folded her hands and pulled them closer to her body, but not before he saw them tremble. His heart lurched. He hadn't meant to upset her. Maybe he shouldn't have come.

She raised her chin. "If you are here to stop me, I'm not listening. We have to stop him—"

"I know." He couldn't force his voice louder than a whisper, but still, she startled. Yeah, maybe it was a mistake to come.

Why was he here, anyway? He thought he had come to stand behind her. To show her that he did believe her...and then convince her to let him go in her place. That way he could prove he trusted her while at the same time protect her. A win-win.

But the shadow of defiance on her face deflated his confidence.

Zane folded his arms. Wow, the guy must like that stance. "We were just talking about how Layla is willing to go into Flint's office—"

Graham inhaled deeply through his nose to stay calm.

"—and where the rest of us will be in case it goes south."

Yeah, breathing deep wasn't working. "And how do we stop it from going south?"

No one answered. They simply stared at him for his stupid question. Of course there was no way to keep it from going south. They all knew it. How could they be okay with a suicide mission?

Arguments building in his throat faded at the look of steel in Layla's eyes. Maybe the best way to protect her was to stand beside her.

Graham scratched the back of his head. "So, what do I do?"

Zane nodded as if he had been hoping Graham would join in. "You know Deputy Dillinger. Get in touch with him and tell him to meet you at the county offices in room… What room did you say, Nora?"

"206."

"Room 206, then wait for Layla to get the confession."

"Like some sort of sidekick." Not what he'd envisioned. "And how will she gain Flint's trust enough to spill? Flint is too smart to play the monologuing villain."

Every eye turned to Layla as if they wanted to know the answer to the same question. She cleared her throat. "By telling Jim that Graham considers me high maintenance. That after getting him buried in the avalanche, he thought I was not worth the drama, so he spurned me."

Her words pounded him the chest. "That isn't true."

She pressed her hands between her knees and focused on an invisible spot on the floor. "It's an excuse for why I want to meet with Flint. I have to convince Jim there is nothing holding me here and I want to make Flint an offer he can't refuse to let me disappear."

Graham huffed. "And what offer could that possibly be?"

"I'm going to say that I scheduled an email with the pictures from Ollie's phone to drop into several prominent inboxes. If they kill me, the emails will be sent. The only one who can stop the pictures from getting out is me."

"And how will you convince him you have copies of the pictures off of Ollie's phone?" Bailey asked, her face almost as skeptical as Graham felt.

"I'll say that I sent the pictures to myself before Jim destroyed the phone."

Graham swallowed the acid building in his throat. "Flint will want proof that you have the pictures. He'll want to see the pictures." Which would mean he'd find out Layla was lying. Probably kill her on the spot.

Layla released a slow exhale. "I hope I can catch his confession before that point."

Was this the point where he locked her in a secure room until she came to her senses? "Cutting it a little close, aren't you?"

Her jaw shifted. "I've been cutting it close for the past two years. God hasn't let me down yet."

With a whimper, Emmy lay her head on her front paws. Graham swung his hand toward Emmy. "See, even Emmy thinks this is risky."

Layla straightened. "I didn't ask you to be here."

"Zane, come on, man. There has to be a better way."

Zane scratched his eyebrow. "If you also tell him

that you have the pictures set to drop on several social media platforms, that might put more pressure on him—meaning he might say things he would normally keep tight lipped about."

"Zane, come on. You can't believe this might work, do you?"

Zane leaned forward in his chair. "Look, Graham, it's a slim shot, but it's still a shot to finally get this guy to confess. A bigger one than we've had yet. Deputy Dillinger will be nearby, and we'll have a distress code if we need to move in." His stare intensified. "I really think this might work."

Might. It might work, or she might be dead. And there was nothing he could do to stop it.

The blood in Graham's healing leg pulsed harder. "I want to be with Dillinger, wherever he'll be." That way, if the distress code was given, he could be the first one on the scene.

Zane grimaced. "I'm not sure if that's a good idea. It's not like you are in the best of shape to be of help if there's trouble. I mean, look at your leg."

"I don't care. I want to be there."

Zane watched Layla for her reaction. She didn't look up, but she did nod.

"Okay, fine. Here's what we are going to do." Zane laid out the assignments.

The others in the room seemed hopeful, but the worst-case scenario scrolled through his head like a twisted movie. Images of Layla lying dead wouldn't leave, her blood staining the snow in some remote location, her body dumped like an old rag doll. But what could he do?

If he demanded she not do this, she would ignore him and do it, anyway. Then hate him even more.

Never had he been so out of control in his entire life. He had to talk to her. Get her alone.

"Layla, can I see you in the kitchen?"

Everyone in the room diverted their attention to him, but he didn't care.

With her chin held high, Layla shoved her way through the kitchen door. As he followed, his crutches cumbersome, the return swing of the door slammed into him.

He pushed through the door as she spun around to meet him with her finger pointed into his chest. "I'm doing this."

Graham glanced down at her finger. "I know."

She straightened. "You know? Then what am I doing in here?"

Graham bent down to look deep into her eyes. "You are really willing to sacrifice your life to get this guy?"

Tears gleamed in her eyes. "Yes."

Graham gripped her shoulders. "Why? Tell me why it is worth your life when I would promise you safety somewhere else? You were the one wanting to run. What changed?"

She tilted her head. "You, Graham." Her voice cracked. "Jim nearly killed you. It made me realize that my testimony, my exposing Flint, may save others. This isn't just about me."

Graham lowered his forehead to hers. "But I wouldn't be able to handle it if I lost you, Layla."

She raised her hands to cradle his cheeks. "I'm also doing this for us. Please, Graham, I need you now. I need you to trust me. To believe in me."

Graham threaded his fingers behind her neck. The wisp of her breath brushed against his lips. "It's so risky."

Her fingers grabbed on to his sweatshirt as if to keep him from pulling away. "I can do this, Graham."

The impulse to stop her didn't ease, but all he could do was promise to be there. Stand beside her. He brushed his lips against her temple. "Okay."

His kiss traveled down her cheek before it hovered over her lips.

She tugged him across the remaining distance until their lips met. So sweet. So full of promise and anticipation.

They could make it through this. They had to.

Because at the end of this long, dark tunnel lay the promise of being together. Of freedom. And of Layla finally coming home for good.

Layla forced away thoughts about tomorrow. No, she must immerse herself in this lie. To pretend she was willing to sell her soul for the chance to escape.

She approached the county government office building on the western edge of town, across from the community center, where it had all began.

The past two days had been a whirlwind of preparation. When she called Jim, she waited for him to finish his string of threats before she asked for an audience with Flint, not leaving out her own threat to tell the sheriff what she'd seen if he didn't follow her request.

She couldn't tell if he bought her story. She would find out in the next few minutes.

Her legs trembled as she rounded the building's corner and pressed her back into the wall. From this angle, she could see Alpha Peak in the distance. Skiers speckled the mountainside, enjoying the warmth of the sun. Each one oblivious that this may be her last day. Oblivious that she existed at all. But it didn't matter.

God saw her. God would give her strength. He had led her back to Silver Ridge for this moment, and she couldn't allow fear to take control. Even if it clamored inside her gut like a cymbal.

She forced a breath before pulling the burner phone Zane had bought for her out of her pocket.

She tapped the only number in the cell's contact list. The person Zane had promised would answer.

"Deputy Dillinger." His voice sounded calm. Almost like he had nothing to lose by giving Graham the benefit of the doubt.

When Graham had contacted Dillinger yesterday, he confessed he had deep suspicions of Flint and eagerly needed a reason to prove them. They weren't recording Flint. Simply using the speakerphone for the purpose of giving Dillinger cause to investigate Flint.

Her breath shuddered over the receiver. "I'm out-side the building."

"We are in position."

She turned on the phone's speaker and hooked the phone into the holster clip on the back of her pants. Then she lowered the hem of her T-shirt over it. She wore a short-enough jacket so that it wouldn't cover the phone. Hopefully, it would work like it did when they tested it.

"Can you still hear me?"

"Ten-four. We hear you."

This was it. "Graham?"

"I'm here, sweetheart. We've got your back."

At the sound of his voice, her eyes slid closed. She loved his voice. Would she hear it again? "Gra-ham—"

Words disappeared. The craving to feel his hand in hers nearly buckled her knees.

"I know," Graham's voice came through the phone. "You can do this."

His reassurance filtered through her doubt, through her fear, and reminded her of why she was doing this. It was for him.

She rounded her shoulders back, lifted her chin and started for the front of the building.

On the sidewalk, Bailey pretended to stretch, dressed in winter jogging gear, appearing com-pletely oblivious to Layla walking by. Emmy and Banner waited patiently at Bailey's side on leashes, although Emmy's eyes followed Layla to the door.

Coby was also somewhere nearby. At least, he should be.

Once in the lobby, the gray tiled floor echoed her footsteps off the cream-colored walls, which were decorated in old historic photographs of Silver Ridge. A few people milled around the area, but they didn't pay her any attention.

She forced a casual pace to the elevator, even though her feet wanted to run. Inside the elevator, she pushed the button for the second floor.

So far, so good. The door opened to an empty second floor. Each door in the corridor remained closed.

As she neared the door Nora had told her to enter, she slowed. She sucked in a long breath before she reached for the doorknob with a cold, clammy hand. Her eyes slid closed for one last prayer before she opened the door.

Inside, Nora sat at a granite-topped desk, typing away at a computer. Formal furniture stood in the waiting room entirely too pristine to sit in. It made Layla look like an invader in her jeans and mukluks.

Without taking her eyes off her computer screen, Nora jerked her head toward the door to the right.

Layla swallowed against the lump in her throat and headed toward the indicated door. She heard male voices inside, but the door muffled the words.

Her pulse drummed in her ears. She opened the door.

Inside, Flint leaned back in his black leather

chair with his fingers steepled in front of him. His jet-black hair was slicked into a stylish wave over his forehead. His expensive suit fit his wide shoulders with a tailored smoothness.

He looked good. Just like he did two years ago. But behind the suave red satin tie lay a dark heart that had never had to pay for his actions. Something Layla fully intended to justify.

He motioned her inside as if welcoming a business partner. "Layla. It's been a while. Come on in."

Jim sat on the edge of Flint's desk, his face not nearly as welcoming as Flint's. Or at least, not as practiced. Instead, he appeared annoyed. Probably annoyed they couldn't just destroy her and be done with it.

But where was Flint's other crony? The one who'd kidnapped her twice?

A shiver traveled down her spine.

Flint gestured to one of the wingback chairs in front of his desk. "Please, take a seat."

"I prefer to stand. Thank you."

Flint nodded. "Jim said you wanted to see me. That you had something for me."

If the man was any more artificial, he'd be made of plastic. "Yes, but first I want your assurance that I can walk out of this office, no strings attached."

"Layla, you make it sound like I wouldn't wish the best for you."

Against every nerve in her body, she stepped closer to his desk to make sure his words sounded clearly into the phone's speaker. "As if you didn't frame me for robbing your office. As if you didn't kill my brother to draw me back to Silver Ridge."

Instead of anger, humor flickered in Flint's eyes. "Oh, Layla. Is that what you really think? Your brother conjured all sorts of conspiracy theories and took some pictures he had no business taking. Then he fell off a cliff."

A light quiver vibrated in her stomach. If she hadn't been kidnapped three times, she'd almost believe Flint.

She pinched her eyes closed and pictured the man she saw murdered two years ago dropping to the ground. Dead.

No, she hadn't imagined it. She needed Flint to confess it, but his tight-lipped smile wasn't about to reveal any secrets. At this rate, Flint would continue to be the model DA in Deputy Matt's eyes.

She straightened, trying to look more confident than she felt. "You mean the pictures that I forwarded to myself from Ollie's phone before Jim shattered it?"

The corner of Flint's smile twitched, but only for a moment. "I don't know what you are talking about."

Jim stood and came closer. "How do we know you have the pictures?"

Layla swallowed. "I've set up an email and social media drop to happen at noon. Only I can stop it. I will stop it if you let me walk away and never look back. You leave me alone, I leave you alone. The pictures will never again see the light of day."

Flint licked his bottom lip as his gaze switched between Layla and Jim.

Her heart rate picked up speed. He wasn't buying it. She had to think fast. "Why would I lie? Would I come in here, knowing what you could do to me, if I didn't have those pictures? What would be the purpose?"

Jim began to circle behind her.

Her breath became audible. She couldn't panic. Not now. "If I didn't have the pictures, I would have just disappeared. I evaded you for two years. I can do so again."

Flint tapped his fingers on the desk. "Which has me asking, why didn't you disappear? Even if you did have the pictures, why not run away again?"

Layla swallowed as Jim stopped behind her. "Like I said, I want to live without having to watch my back."

Jim grabbed her shoulder, his fingers digging into her flesh. "You are not very bright, girlie." He yanked the cell phone off her pants. He held it up for Flint to see.

Flint rounded his desk and took the phone from Jim's hand. His eyes narrowed.

With a sneer, he tapped the red disconnect button. Numbness settled over her as Deputy Dillinger's number disappeared from the screen.

"There are no pictures, are there, Layla?"

Layla couldn't move. She heard the words, but they didn't register, as if she was watching the scene from somewhere else in the room.

Flint licked his lower lip. "Jim, take Layla for a walk."

A one-way walk. Based on their conversation, Dillinger didn't have any evidence to believe she was in danger.

Jim's face revealed no emotion, but his shoulders stiffened. "Boss, I—"

"You buried your friend in an avalanche. You can finish this job."

"I think it's a mistake—"

Flint slammed his fist on the desk. "My mistake was believing that I could count on you. If I can't count on you, you become obsolete. You know what happens to people who are obsolete."

Jim's face paled, and he pulled out a gun from beneath his jacket.

A slow sneer shadowed Flint's face. "No chances of her surviving. This time, point-blank." He turned cold, calculating eyes to Jim. "I'll just pin it on some other poor sap."

Layla swayed. She almost fell over until Jim caught her arm, then led her out the door.

SEVENTEEN

Graham turned cold when the line went dead. Something had gone wrong. The printer room Nora had rushed them into only an hour ago began to spin.

He slammed his fist into the arm of the office chair he sat in. "Call her back?"

Dillinger stared at the phone. "We can't just call her. Not with Flint in the room."

Graham planted his crutches in front of him. He needed to go to her. See with his own eyes what was happening in that room next to theirs.

He heaved his body out of the chair and balanced himself on his crutches. "Fine. Let's go."

Deputy Dillinger ran a hand down his face. "I can't storm in there, guns blazing, Graham. If we go in there, Flint will just keep up his act. We gained nothing."

Nothing. No confession. No hints of probable cause.

Using his earpiece, Dillinger called to Bailey and Coby, but they didn't answer. Had someone found them out? If so, their whole operation was over.

A growl rumbled in his chest. If he waited for backup, they'd lose her trail. He was leaving now.

Graham shoved his chair out of his way. Dillinger's voice trailed behind him, but he didn't stop to listen. Besides, the pulse in his ears drowned out the words.

Flint's door came into view. He rounded a nearby corner and pressed himself into the wall, trying hard not to let his casted leg bang against anything.

Dillinger sidled up next to him. "Wait for backup."

"Not on your life. Bailey and Coby went silent." The *why* worried him.

Dillinger stopped his reply when Flint's door opened, and Jim led Layla out. His fake friend's face was almost as pale as Layla's. Whatever had happened in the office left both shaken.

Graham ignored the sickness in his gut. "Go get help. I'll follow them."

"I'm the law. I'll follow them."

As if he was going to let Layla out of his sight. "But you are faster and have connections. I can keep watch from a distance and alert you as to which direction they go. I have my cell."

"No, Graham, that is not—"

Graham ignored Dillinger and hobbled out of his hiding spot, following them down the stairs and out a side door.

Jim kept his hands in the pockets of his coat. Probably concealing a weapon pointed into Layla's back, by the way she marched forward with stiff focus.

At a discreet pace, almost warily, Jim crossed the street and moved through the community center's parking lot toward a wilderness area beyond.

Graham stayed far behind, tracking their footprints in the muddy snow through the forest along a hidden trail. One that looked underused and forgotten.

His leg throbbed and his underarms chafed. He should probably stop and call Dillinger, but Graham kept going, desperate to find Layla.

After only a few yards, the two sets of prints veered off the path and into the woods.

Graham stiffened his jaw and followed. His crutches sank deep into the snow, slowing his pace, but his pulse thrummed for him to hurry. Still, he couldn't move any faster.

The sound of rushing water filtered through the thick pines, masking all other sound. After a few paces forward, the stream came into view. As did Jim, standing over Layla, who was kneeling, the gun pointed directly at her head.

Tears streamed out of her eyes. She looked resolute, not fearful.

Graham didn't have time to wait for Matt's backup. Not with a gun to Layla's head.

He clenched his crutches. Stupid leg. He could take Jim. He was faster, stronger, but with a bum leg, Graham was target practice before Jim turned and shot Layla.

He needed to be fast, and he couldn't be. He needed to be strong, but how strong could he be when he was leaning on crutches for balance?

His crutches. He may be a good distance from Jim, but it was all he had.

Graham shoved one of the crutches deep into the snow. He would need two hands on the crutch. Then he lifted it over his shoulder like a baseball bat.

He stepped out of the trees. "Jim, don't."

Jim startled and he redirected his gun toward Graham. Graham winced, but the gun didn't discharge. Yet.

"Don't come any closer, Graham. I'll shoot her. I'm going to anyway, but I'd rather not shoot you too."

Graham saw it then—the torment on Jim's face. The tremble in his arm as he held the gun.

He looked, well, afraid.

Graham lowered his crutch. "Jim, you don't want to do this."

"It isn't a matter of want, Graham. I don't have a choice."

Graham hopped closer until he stood in front of Jim. The fact that a bullet had yet to pierce him was a good sign. "Yes, you do. You don't have to work for Flint."

"Graham, what are you doing? You'll just get killed too." Layla's voice trembled.

Jim narrowed his eyes. "I'm in too deep, Graham. This is about survival."

Graham leaned onto his crutch. The throb in

his leg intensified. "There are better ways to pay for your mom's treatments, Jim. Your testimony against Flint would make you a hero. Especially to your mom."

Jim clenched and unclenched his jaw. Then he swung the gun to point directly at Layla's head again. She sucked in a breath.

Jim's arm quaked. "No jury in the world would convict him. He's too careful. Too trusted. I have to carry this through."

"Jim, listen to me. Between you and Layla's testimony, a jury would have to pay attention."

Jim gnawed at his trembling lip. "This has gone too far."

"Yes. Yes, it has."

A rustling out of the woods made Graham flinch. He swung his crutch back over his shoulder.

The man who had tried to kidnap Layla stepped out of the trees, his hands in the air. A small streak of satisfaction passed through Graham at the sight of the fading bruise he'd delivered by the shovel.

"What the—" Jim's gaze flitted between the newcomer and Layla, the gun pointed toward her head shaking. "What are you doing here?"

Unease crawled through Graham's gut. What was going on? Every muscle tingled with tension.

A sneer lifted the corner of the newcomer's mouth. "Becoming a witness."

With swift reflexes, the man reached into his pocket, but he didn't pull out a gun. He pulled out a camera.

"Say cheese." He took a picture of Jim standing over Layla before anyone could respond. "Beautiful. Just what Flint needs to put you in jail."

Jim seethed, his shoulders rising and falling in fast succession. "You backstabbing—"

With a growl, he launched toward the man, tackling him to the ground. Fists from both men hit their targets. Grunts mixed in with the rush of the stream.

Graham hurried over to Layla, struggling against his crutch catching in the snow. He finally reached her and helped her to her feet.

"What's happening?" she asked, her voice trembling.

"None of our concern. Let's go."

With her under his arm, they started back to the path, but Graham's broken leg slowed their escape.

A gunshot burst through the air, followed by Jim's cry behind them. Layla flinched beneath his arm, and his gut lurched. But they couldn't stop. Not if they didn't want to be the next victims.

"Keep going!"

They only made it two more strides when a bullet spewed into the pine next to them, spraying them in splintered wood.

"Stop before I kill you both."

Graham felt Layla's shudder in his core, and they slowly turned around.

The sight of Jim bleeding into the snow caused Layla's stomach to convulse. Still conscious, Jim gripped his shoulder, moaning. Never had she imagined Flint's cronies turning on each other.

Graham shifted the one crutch under his arm, like he wanted to find a way to use it as a weapon.

The other man's gun didn't quake. "Now, come here."

Graham hesitated, but then, as if deciding they couldn't outrun a bullet, he guided her to obey.

The man motioned toward Graham. "That's real good. Now let her go and stand here."

Graham drew in a long breath, his eyes narrowing. The man was obviously up to something, but Graham did as he was told.

Once close enough, the man pulled a cloth from his coat, wiped off the gun and then pressed it into Graham's hand.

"Take it, and I might convince Flint to let your sweetheart go."

Layla shook her head, a scream gathering in her gut. She couldn't speak over the lump in her throat. All she could utter was "No."

Without turning toward her, Graham's throat bobbed once before he gripped the gun in his hand.

Layla's knees nearly buckled. Why did he have such a need to protect her?

Footsteps approached from the trail.

Layla spun to see Flint stepping out from the trees, followed closely by two sheriffs.

Layla gasped, trying to control the surge of panic.

"Nice work, Thomas." Flint motioned toward

Graham, his face pretending revulsion at the scene in front of him. "You caught them. What did I tell you, Officer? These are the criminals who broke into my office and have now become violent. Probably knew we were onto them."

Layla's breath rushed out of her lungs. "I didn't steal anything."

But the officer ignored her and nodded toward Jim. "And this guy?"

A smile slithered across Flint's mouth. "He's one of them. Looks like a criminal spat. Arrest them all."

"Wait!" Jim bellowed, his face livid. "How can you do this to me?"

Flint's brow lifted with mock concern. "What are you talking about? You are the one who decided to work with criminals."

Jim paled.

Graham threw the gun into the snow. "Wait a minute—"

"You are under arrest." One of the officers started toward them while the other unholstered his gun.

Acid stirred in Layla's stomach. "No! You've got it all wrong."

She moved to stand between the officers and Graham. Graham twisted to reach for her arm, but grimaced and gripped his leg. "Layla, stop."

She sucked in a breath and pointed at Flint. "He's the guy who's been trying to kill me for the past two years."

The officer ignored her and stepped behind Graham. The other reached for Layla.

No, this couldn't be happening. "We didn't do anything wrong."

Her gaze flitted between the officer's and Flint, nearly hyperventilating.

"Stop!"

Deputy Dillinger appeared out of the forest with Bailey and Coby close behind, holding tight to Banner and Emmy on leashes. Layla's knees almost buckled.

Emmy started barking, pulling hard against her restraints.

Coby shot a look toward the officers. "They aren't the ones you need to arrest. Ask Flint. He just detained us for falsified reasons."

"You will have to leave," said one of the officers, shouting over Emmy's barking.

Bailey used two hands on the leash to restrain Emmy, who now jumped and yanked against her restraints. "He's telling the truth. Emmy, quiet."

Layla put her hand toward Emmy. "Hush, Emmy. We'll be okay." But Emmy pulled harder, launching her body from side to side.

"Hold tight to that leash, Bailey!" Graham shouted.

"Emmy, quiet!" If Emmy got away and bit one of the officers, they would euthanize her for being aggressive. But Bailey was losing her grip.

"Emmy, hush. It's okay!" Graham shouted over the chaos.

But it was too late. Emmy's leash ripped out of Bailey's hand. At full speed, Emmy raced toward Layla.

The officer pointed the barrel of his gun toward at Emmy. "Call your dog off!"

"Emmy, wait!" Layla's shout weakened as Emmy ran past her to a mound of snow behind Jim and began sniffing.

Jim struggled to his feet, his eyes wide as Emmy began to dig.

"What is she doing?" one of the officers demanded.

Flint rushed forward. "This is ridiculous. Why are we standing here watching a dog dig through the snow? Can we get on with this please?"

"You lying bag of—" But Graham froze.

So did Layla, because Flint's face had become ashen. So ashen he looked like he might be sick.

Then, one piece at a time, the confident mask Flint always wore cracked and fell away, revealing unconcealed rage.

He charged toward Emmy.

"No!" Jim stepped between Flint and Emmy, his hand gripping his bloody shoulder. "Let's see what she finds, shall we?"

An ugly sneer crossed Flint's mouth. "You ungrateful fool."

Emmy's paws stopped digging, and she began yanking on something beneath the dirt.

Jim's nostrils flared. "Ungrateful, Flint? Ungrateful that you were about to turn on me?"

From beneath the ground, Emmy withdrew a bone. Not just any bone, but a human femur.

One of the officers leaned over to examine it. "What in the world…"

Jim stood straighter. A look of resolution fell across his face. "That is the man I buried two years ago because Cameron Flint killed him before my eyes. I always felt guilty, so I buried him in a shallow grave, hoping he'd be found."

A hush fell across the group. Everyone seemed to be assessing each other, analyzing the truth. Could these be the remains of Zane's friend, Ryan Murphey?

Flint straightened, his plastic smile back. "Who are you going to believe? Me or him?"

Dillinger placed his hand on the hilt of his gun, a satisfied smile on his face. "Why are you acting so nervous, Mr. Flint?"

Oxygen returned to Layla's lungs in a rush. This was her chance to speak truth. To do what she should've done a long time ago.

She turned toward Graham and their gazes locked. He gave her a silent nod.

Without tearing her eyes from his, Layla said with boldness, "I was there. Two years ago, I witnessed Cameron Flint kill a man."

EIGHTEEN

Layla gripped the doorknob in her hand, inhaling the air of home. Bliss coursed through every limb. With a swell of joy, she turned the handle and stepped outside.

Yep, her bungalow. Her home. The one left for her in Ollie's will.

She'd finished signing the paperwork that morning and it was official. With a steady hand, she'd signed the deed, then lingered on the last loop of her name, savoring its satisfaction.

Home.

Standing on the welcome doormat with the adorable dog holding a bone in its mouth, she closed her eyes, and breathed.

It was over. Well, mostly.

Based on her and Jim's testimonies, Cameron Flint, district attorney, was stripped of his position and indicted for his corruption. The upcoming trial would be grueling, but she knew that with God, she'd be brave enough to tell her story in front of the jury and judge.

Jim would also serve time, but Dillinger told

Layla that he received a hefty plea deal for his testimony.

A car drove down the street—her street with her home on it—and spewed the spring slush from the road up over the sidewalk. Layla looked at her watch. She could bask in this new stage later. If she didn't hurry, she would be late.

Graham had told her to meet him after his shift at the base of the slopes to celebrate tomorrow's move-in day.

He'd been cleared for work earlier that week, although only to man the lifts. But the doctor had assured him that his leg should be ready to hit the slopes again next season. This season only had a week left before the lifts closed, anyway.

In the aftermath of all the chaos, they'd spent the quality time Layla craved, even if only in fragments.

She boarded the gondola with the after-hours crowd making it to the base of Alpha Peak. The lodges at the base always promised good music and good food. That is, if the skier wanted to shell out a pretty penny.

At the top, music drifted from the condominium as she stepped off the gondola and strolled through the bustling skiers coming down from the slopes. Many headed for the gondola, but many also headed toward one of the fine restaurants.

A few of the patrol members walked by her on their way home, a slight wave from some of them.

Layla wandered the base. No Graham. As she came toward the Breezeway Lift, Zane waved and called her over.

Layla approached him. "Hey, Zane, where's Graham? I thought I was supposed to meet him here."

Zane jerked his head toward the mountain. "He hasn't come down yet."

"Hasn't come down? Aren't the slopes closed?"

"He's waiting for you."

Layla glanced up at the slope glowing orange in the setting sun. "I'm confused."

A sly smile crossed Zane's lip. "He's at the top of the lift. I promised I'd man it until you two came down."

"I'm still confused."

Zane chuckled. "Then go up there and ask him."

Layla narrowed her eyes, but Zane ignored her scrutiny and swung his arm toward the lift. "Go, will ya?"

Obviously, Zane refused to squeal, so she plopped into the chair and waited for it to take her up the mountain.

With spring on the horizon, the late-afternoon sun sat above the ridge, coating the surface of the snow with gold.

The lift came to the top, and Layla hopped off, scanning the vacant slope for Graham. Then she saw it. A rose petal. Then another.

A trail of rose petals created a path up to the top of the ridge.

A smile forced its way across Layla's face. She covered it with her hand.

She didn't hurry as she followed the trail of rose petals. No, she needed to savor every detail.

When the trees cleared, the expanse of mountains stretched over the horizon, the setting sun casting every hue imaginable.

Layla gasped. The view was breathtaking. But it wasn't the view that made her gasp. It was Graham.

He stood in the clearing, in a black coat that was unzipped far enough to reveal a royal blue silk tie and a white collared shirt. His hair was parted straight down the middle and hung in neat curls grazing the top of his collar. His hands hung at his sides, and his smile wobbled a little as she approached.

Beside him stood Emmy with a big red bow tied around her neck. In her mouth, she carried a black silk bag of some sort.

A small laugh escaped her throat. "Graham, what is this?"

He exhaled as if he'd been holding his breath. "I'm glad you came."

She drew close enough for his warmth to embrace her. "I will always show up for you, Graham. You know that."

His gaze intensified as he took her hands in his. "Layla, words will never be able to express my love for you."

"You don't have to, Graham. I don't need eloquent words."

He glanced down at their entwined hands. "I know you've been through a lot. We've been through a lot. But I love you more with each passing day."

"I love you, Graham." Her throat closed off as she said his name, making it come out in a squeak.

Graham nodded, but he didn't look up. Instead, the muscle in his jaw flexed once, then twice. Emmy let out a little whine.

Graham looked down and patted her on her head. "Okay, girl."

He took the bag from Emmy's mouth and pulled out a diamond ring embraced by icy-blue sapphires.

Everything stilled around her.

Graham held the ring so she could see it. "Layla, this is my grandmother's ring that I had restored. For you, actually."

Layla's voice refused to cooperate.

"Forgive me for not getting down on one knee. My brace makes me move like an old man."

Layla's heart raced. "Yes."

His brow crinkled.

"Oh, I didn't mean that. I'm sorry. I jumped ahead. Go on."

He took her hand in his and slid on the ring. "Layla, will you marry me?"

The ring wrapped around her finger perfectly. Like it belonged. She sniffed. "Yes."

He slid his arms around her waist. "I love you, Layla Quin."

Then he lowered his lips to hers in a kiss that welcomed her home.

* * * * *

Dear Reader,

Thank you for reading my debut story with Love Inspired Suspense!

This story started when my family adopted our own black Labrador puppy, Molly, who has huge floppy ears and a playful spirit. While out with Molly, a friend shared a heartwarming story about his own black Lab saving a lost little girl while camping, sparking my fascination with rescue dogs.

Both Graham and Layla have been wounded by those they trusted the most. Sometimes, those closest to us can inflict the deepest pain, but God never abandons us. He never leaves us, nor forsakes us.

If you would like to see pictures of Molly or hear of my upcoming books, please visit www.tracisummeril.com, and if you'd like, sign up for my newsletter. I would love to connect with you!

Blessings!
Teresa Summers aka *Traci Summeril*

HARLEQUIN
Reader Service

Enjoyed your book?

Try the perfect subscription for Romance readers and get more great books like this delivered right to your door.

See why over 10+ million readers have tried Harlequin Reader Service.

Start with a Free Welcome Collection with free books and a gift—valued over $20.

Choose any series in print or ebook.
See website for details and order today:

TryReaderService.com/subscriptions